No More School

'I feel thick at school. The other kids tease me 'cos I live on a boat. You always have to do what the teachers say, even if you think it's really stupid… I just hate it.'

Flora loves living on a canal boat, but she loathes school. So her best friend Joss covers for her when she bunks off. Then something happens to change everything—Flora makes a new friend, Tan. And soon she has a very big secret.

Meanwhile, Joss becomes strangely distant and preoccupied. Is she jealous of Tan? Or is there something more sinister going on?

Former teacher Meg Harper is married with four children, whom she educates at home. As well as writing, she enjoys reading, history, swimming and roller-blading. Her two other books *My Mum and Other Horror Stories* and *Cyberpest* are also published by Lion.

For Caroline and Alis

No More School

Meg Harper

LION
Children's Books

Text copyright © 1998 Meg Harper
This edition copyright © 1998 Lion Publishing

The author asserts the moral right to be
identified as the author of this work

Published by
Lion Publishing plc
Sandy Lane West, Oxford, England
www.lion-publishing.co.uk
ISBN 0 7459 3963 5

First edition 1998
10 9 8 7 6 5 4 3 2 1

A catalogue record for this book is available
from the British Library

Typeset in 11/13 Garamond ITC Light BT
Printed and bound in Great Britain by
Cox & Wyman, Reading

1

Scratch! Scratch! Scratch!

Silence. Joss paused and looked about her. Everything was still. No sign of anyone, anywhere.

Then she heard it again. Scratch! Scratch! Scratch! Scratch! Scratch!

'Flora!' she called. 'I know you're there somewhere. I can hear you. Come on out. Your mum wants you for your tea!'

High up on the canal bank a tree rustled, and two bony, blotchy legs appeared before their owner dropped down and slithered to meet Joss. She was small and blonde and sulky.

'Flora!' gasped Joss in horror, seeing the angry red patches of rash round Flora's wrists and knees. 'You really shouldn't scratch it, you know. I could hear you miles away!'

'No, you couldn't.'

'Could too.'

Flora glowered at her friend. 'Well, you'd scratch too if you'd got eczema like mine. I can't help it. And it's been really terrible today.'

'Well, it certainly is now,' agreed Joss. 'School bad then, was it?'

Flora looked away. 'I couldn't stand it after yesterday,' she said. 'I bunked off.'

5

'Oh, Flora!' wailed Joss. 'Not again! I can't *keep* writing notes for you! Someone'll work it out. And what's your mum going to say if she finds out?'

Flora shrugged and set off along the tow-path, her shoulders hunched.

Joss hurried after her. What on earth was to be done about Flora? School couldn't be that bad, could it? Not so bad that it brought you out in horrible, itchy eczema and gave you migraine attacks? Not so bad that you'd rather bunk off and walk the two miles home? Joss had always quite liked school herself. It was a bit boring, of course, and she was always glad to get back in the afternoon, but she'd never been worried about going—not like Flora.

Flora trudged along miserably. She could guess what Joss was thinking. Joss was the only real friend she'd got—but for how long? She was eleven—a year older than Flora. She'd be at secondary school before long. What did she want with a terrified little mouse of a friend like Flora, all covered in disgusting, scaly eczema? Joss was easy-going and exotic and beautiful. She didn't need Flora. Not like Flora needed her. If Joss ever—and it was hardly likely—wanted to bunk off, she would have to write her own notes. Flora couldn't do them.

It wasn't long till they were home. Flora's mum was standing on the tow-path talking to Joss' dad, Reuben. Her body was stiff. There was going to be trouble.

'Thank you, Joscelyn,' she said, tersely. 'I'm sorry to have had to bother you.'

Flora ducked down past her and clambered onto their narrow boat, the *Thorpe Cloud*. In the dim interior her mum might not notice that she'd been scratching.

'S'all right,' said Joss. 'Can Flora come over after tea?

6

Our band's jamming later. You could come too if you're not busy.' Joss flashed Flora's mum a winning smile.

'Do,' said Reuben, warmly. 'It's been a while since you've joined us, Libby.'

Flora's mum ran a hand along her brow, tiredly. 'Yes, I know,' she said. 'If I finish my work early, I'll come. It's just that I've been very busy these last few weeks. But at least it means some money's coming in.'

Then she followed Flora along the gangplank which joined the *Thorpe Cloud* to the canal tow-path. Joss and her father climbed aboard their narrow boat, which was moored alongside.

'I suppose you know I nearly go out of my wits when you disappear like this?' snapped Flora's mum, as she banged a plate down in front of her. 'When you're finished at school, you're to come straight here and tell me. How many times do you need to be told? As if there wasn't enough to worry about, bringing you up on my own, without you playing silly tricks like that! For all I knew, you might have been at the bottom of the canal!'

'I can swim,' said Flora, stonily, pulling down the cuffs of her shirt before she picked up her fork. If her mum saw the state of her wrists there would only be more trouble.

'Well, you might have been abducted!' retorted Libby.

'What's that mean?'

'You know. A strange person might have taken you away.'

'Oh,' said Flora. That old scare story again. Well, she'd just have to make sure she was very careful when she bunked off school. Not speak to any strangers and all that. Not that she would, anyway.

They continued to eat in silence. Flora was never very

7

chatty at the best of times and Libby was cross and tired. She worked as a freelance writer and was struggling to meet a deadline for a magazine story. Flora going missing like that had wasted a valuable hour. It would be a relief to pack her off next door for the evening— though it would have been even nicer to go herself.

The sound of instruments being tuned drifted in through the open portholes.

'Can I go, Mum?' demanded Flora, eagerly.

'Oh yes, go on then,' said Libby, wearily. 'I'll do the washing-up myself.' *Bother*, she thought privately. She'd forgotten that in good weather the musicians tended to spill out onto the tow-path. It would be even more diffi-cult to concentrate now. Not for the first time Libby wondered whether it really was such a good idea to live on a narrow boat. But at least it cost less than a house.

'Hi there, Flora-Dora!' called Reuben, as Flora emerged from the cabin. 'Glad you decided to come. Can I persuade you to join in this evening? Perhaps a tambourine or a drum?'

Flora shook her head, shyly. 'I'll just listen, thanks,' she said and wandered over to where Joss was fiddling with her flute.

'You gonna play tonight, then?' she asked.

Joss nodded. 'Just a bit. Where I don't have to impro-vise.'

'What's that mean?'

'Make it up as we go along,' said Joss, with a laugh.

Flora shook her head dumbly. Joss and her family were amazing. One of the things they did for a living was to play in a folk band. Weekends were usually busy with barn dances and hoedowns. In the week Reuben went off down the tow-path on his bike to work at the

8

boat yard. What he didn't know about the old wooden narrow boats wasn't worth knowing. His wife, Zilla, painted wonderful kettles and jugs and plates, all decorated with brightly coloured castles and roses, just like everyone used once on the canals. She sold them to all the tourists who cruised up and down in rented boats. But for three days a week she disappeared off to town to work as a herbalist.

'What's that mean?' Flora had asked.

'I help people to get better with my herbs.'

'How?' demanded Flora.

'I make drinks with them—that sort of thing,' explained Zilla.

'Could you make my eczema better?' asked Flora.

'Maybe,' said Zilla. 'But your mum would have to agree.'

Flora sighed. She knew what Libby thought of Zilla. All along the roof of their narrow boat were painted pots and trays of herbs, which everyone was strictly forbidden to touch. 'They're powerful things are herbs,' said Zilla, darkly.

'I think it's safer to stick to the proper doctor,' said Libby, uncomfortably.

Flora sighed. The proper doctor hadn't got rid of her eczema. All his creams helped but none of them got rid of it. She looked at Joss' beautiful, pale wrists as she held her flute to her lips and then looked at her own, red and blotchy and covered in ointment. If she could just be like Joss in one small way, she would be happy. But it was no good. She would always be small and mousy and stupid, she was sure. She couldn't even read properly, let alone play a musical instrument. She knew she was a big disappointment to her mum. Perhaps her

9

dad had been stupid. But Libby never talked about him.

But it was silly to waste a lovely June evening being gloomy. The music was livening up and people were beginning to drift down from the pub by the bridge to listen and even to dance. Flora watched, entranced. She was never bored when there were people to watch.

When the light began to go Flora shivered and crawled back into the boat to fetch her sleeping-bag. Libby was still hunched over her typewriter and didn't speak. Soon Flora was huddled up on the bank in her bag with a mug of hot chocolate provided by Zilla. Lulled by the music and the warmth of her drink, her head sank back on the grass and she fell asleep.

'Dad!' said Joss, nodding in the direction of Flora, and Reuben put down his fiddle. He was a big man and he scooped up the sleeping bundle easily. Within moments he had climbed aboard the *Thorpe Cloud* and snuggled Flora down on her bed. He had done it before. Libby didn't even look up.

'Poor little mite,' said Reuben to himself.

It was Saturday the next day and both Flora and Libby slept late. They woke to a warm, drizzly day, but neither of them minded. Libby was jubilant to have finished her story and Flora was happy anywhere as long as it wasn't school.

'Let's go for a long tramp through the fields and then come home and make fudge,' said Libby enthusiastically, after breakfast. 'I've got to do something for the church bring-and-buy sale and we're good at fudge.'

Flora beamed her approval and ran to find her wellies. It sounded like her idea of a perfect day—fresh air, peace and quiet... and sweeties at the end of it.

They had a lovely time, getting thoroughly damp and muddy on the overgrown footpaths which laced their way through the fields. It wasn't until Flora was stirring the fudge that Libby noticed her wrists.

'Flora! Your eczema!' Libby cried as, too late, Flora tried to pull down her sleeves. 'Why didn't you tell me it was bad again?'

Flora shrugged. It was only three weeks since the last time it had flared up badly.

'Maybe it's the weather,' she said, apologetically.

'Hmm,' said her mum, grimly. 'A likely story.'

Sunday was lovely too, apart from when Libby insisted on going to church. This was quite a novelty. A few months ago a new vicar had come to the village and he'd made a lot of changes. Libby had been impressed. He had come to visit her on the *Thorpe Cloud*, even though she'd never been to the church. She had decided to try out a church service and had surprised herself by enjoying it. Now she went nearly every week. Flora steadfastly refused to go. She knew about the village church. It had a Sunday School—and she wasn't going near anything that might be connected with school. So that hour and a half was now spent with Joss, whose family weren't at their best on a Sunday morning, having usually been out with the band the night before.

But the afternoon was wonderful. They spent most of it curled up together whilst Libby read out loud. They were reading *A Little Princess*. Flora shuddered at the thought of being sent away to school like Sara Crewe, the heroine. She was lost in admiration for her ability to make the little children love her. *If only*, Flora thought longingly. *If only*.

11

* * *

And then it was Monday again and Flora woke with the familiar sick feeling in the pit of her stomach. School. Fretfully, her fingers picked at the scabby places on her wrists and then she leaped off her bed before she could make them any worse.

'I must not scratch, I must not scratch,' she repeated to herself as she scrambled into her clothes. Perhaps one day she would teach her stupid brain not to want to.

2

'Oh, I forgot to tell you,' said Libby, as she ladled out plates of bean stew.

'Forgot to tell me what?' asked Flora, half-heartedly. She just hoped it wasn't something awful like school going on a week longer than she'd thought, or her teacher wanting to see Libby. Right at this moment she was blissfully happy. She'd just watched 'Blue Peter', a high spot of her week—the generator on the *Thorpe Cloud* didn't stand up to too much television watching.

'There's some people moved into that big, old house just beyond the lock. They were at church,' continued Libby.

'You mean Buxton House?' Flora's interest was immediate. Shy as she was, people fascinated her, especially those who lived along the canal. 'But it's all falling apart.'

'Oh, it's not that bad. Needs the windows replacing, I shouldn't wonder, and a lot of work to make it nice inside, but it's perfectly habitable.'

'So what are they like? Are there any kids?' demanded Flora. She wasn't sure she wanted more kids living along the canal, but when Joss went off to secondary school maybe she'd need someone else.

'Well, that's the strange thing,' said Libby, settling down to her stew. 'It seems it's only a chap with one little boy—about your age he looked, or maybe a bit older. Just the two of them in that huge house. Seems a bit odd to me.'

'Were they nice?' Flora asked, wistfully, playing with her fork.

'How should I know? I didn't get a chance to speak to them. I just saw them across the church and, of course, everyone was talking about them.'

'Oh,' said Flora, and wondered. A man and his son in that big, old house that Flora had longed and longed to explore and had never quite dared. Perhaps the boy's mum had gone off, like Flora's dad had. Or perhaps she had died. Perhaps the man was only the boy's guardian. Perhaps they were incredibly famous and had come here to hide away from it all. Dreamily, Flora scooped stew into her mouth and chewed, whilst in her imagination she wove wonderful histories for the man and the boy at Buxton House.

'Wake up, Flora! I said, "Do you want fruit or a yoghurt?"' Libby's voice broke the spell.

'Oh, an apple, please.' Flora's dream of a child film star and his jealously protective father curled up and died.

'I didn't see him on the school bus,' she said, puzzled.

'Who?'

'The boy from Buxton House, of course.'

'So maybe he goes to a private school. They can't be poor. Buxton House may be run down but it isn't exactly small.'

'Hmm…' said Flora, thoughtfully. Perhaps he really was a child star. Perhaps he had his very own drama tutor and a governess for all the other stuff. Flora adored the idea of a governess. It would be so wonderful to be able to learn in the peace and quiet of home, without

14

the noise and clutter of thirty other kids around you and with one kind, patient grown-up, ready and willing to help you when you didn't understand.

She picked up her apple.

'Can I go for a quick walk?' she asked. 'I'll do the drying-up when I come back.'

'On your own, or with Joss?'

'Oh, just by myself.'

Libby looked surprised. 'Well, all right,' she said. 'But not past Buxton Tunnel, OK?'

Flora beamed. That was exactly what she had thought Libby would say. It suited her fine. Buxton House was just their side of the tunnel.

It was a beautiful evening. Flora ran along the tow-path light-heartedly. The cool evening air soothed her eczema which had tortured her all day in the warmth of the classroom. It almost covered her arms and had begun to spread to her face. She met no one and no boat passed her. The canal only grew busy later in the season and at weekends. It would be easy to slip into the grounds of Buxton House unnoticed.

It was obvious, even from the gate to the tow-path, that someone had arrived. Where there had been a dense jungle of ancient rhododendrons, a path had been clipped clear and Flora could peer along to where it joined a circle of weed-covered gravel outside the front door. A very ordinary-looking estate car was parked amid the weeds and through the open door Flora could hear a radio. She had to admit that it didn't look like film-star territory. But maybe it was all part of the cover. A flashy car and security guards would give the game away at once.

Flora crept along the path. At the edge of the gravel

15

she glanced around and then, greatly daring, darted across it and up the two steps onto the porch. She listened intently for a moment and then backed down the steps. It sounded for all the world like home. Someone was busy in the kitchen and listening to the radio. Maybe it was the child star's housekeeper.

Stealthily, Flora tiptoed round the corner of the house. The first window was high up and small—a cloakroom, perhaps. But the next room might be the kitchen. The radio was louder here and Flora thought she could smell cooking. The window-ledge was high and Flora didn't dare pull herself up to peer in. But there was a rusty old dustbin on the far side of the window. If she climbed up on that she could probably get a quick look in without being seen.

Never for a moment did it occur to Flora to march up to the front door, lift the huge knocker and introduce herself. That was the sort of thing she left to Joss and, once Flora had sussed this place out, she might persuade her to come and do it. But Flora would sooner have died.

For now, she was content with crawling past the window, finding a couple of old bricks to use as a step up and perching precariously on top of the dustbin. It was very wobbly up there. She had to cling to the cracks in the brickwork to keep her balance, but was rewarded with a clear view into the kitchen.

Inside was a man cooking pancakes. He looked like an expert. As he finished each pancake he flipped it neatly onto an ever-growing pile, stacked on a plate over a steaming pan. The kitchen looked as if it hadn't been cooked in for fifty years, except that the table had been freshly scrubbed. Laid out on it was a dish of quartered lemons, a sugar bowl and a group of matching bowls, the sort that Libby drooled over longingly in trendy kitchen shops and never had the money to buy.

Flora gazed through the window wistfully. She thought of the cluttered meals she had with her mum, usually in a hurriedly cleared space in the middle of her work, and the way they had to scrabble round in the bursting cupboards if they suddenly wanted vinegar or ketchup in the middle of a meal. For a moment she wanted to cry and then felt horribly disloyal. It wasn't her mum's fault they had to live in such a small, cramped space. And he couldn't be a very nice man even if he was ace at pancakes (Libby claimed to have a horror of people who fussed about keeping things neat and tidy). 'A tidy house is the sign of a misspent life,' she would say firmly. 'There are far more important things to do than tidy up.'

But, secretly, Flora longed for a tidy bit of space to call her own.

'Excuse me…' The voice came without warning.

Flora, eyes on the pancake man, clutched at the window-sill in alarm and lost her balance. With a great clatter the bin fell over and she promptly landed on top of it.

'Oh crikey, I'm sorry. Here…' The next moment a thin, scruffily-dressed boy had yanked her to her feet.

'What's going on?' It was the pancake man calling.

'It's OK, Dad. Just the bin falling over.'

Flora brushed herself down. The boy, who was somewhat taller than her and very tanned, watched, an anxious frown on his friendly face. 'Why didn't you tell him?' she gasped, unsteadily. She felt sore all over and had banged her head, but she wasn't going to cry in front of this strange boy.

'You didn't want him to know you were here,' the boy hissed. 'Why should I tell him?'

'But I...' She broke off, confused. Most of the kids that Flora knew were only too glad to get each other into trouble. 'I don't know,' she said, lamely.

'Are you badly hurt?' demanded the boy. 'Is there any blood?'

Flora shook her head.

'Good,' the boy nodded. 'Then come with me.'

Flora hesitated, unsure of what to do. It seemed rude to refuse, but where was he going to take her?

'Come on!' said the boy. 'What are you waiting for?'

Bemused, Flora did as she was told. Suddenly everything seemed rather unreal. Warily, she followed the boy across what must have once been a lawn and along an overgrown path through more rhododendron bushes. They emerged by some long, broken cold frames and a couple of low brick sheds.

The boy opened the door of the second shed.

'My den,' he said, proudly, and beckoned Flora in. 'I've still got a lot to do, but I've made a start. Sit down.'

Again, Flora did as she was told. She perched uneasily on the edge of a huge wing-backed armchair, which took up a large part of the tiny room. Most of the rest was taken up by a tall, old-fashioned desk with its own built-in seat, the sort you might see in a museum. The desk was piled high with sheets of paper of all shapes and sizes and on the dusty, narrow shelves above it was a great clutter of paint pots, brushes, felt-tipped pens, crayons and odd-shaped clay ornaments.

'I'm having a sort-out,' said the boy, helpfully, and sat sideways on the desk seat so he was facing her.

Flora looked out of the window nervously, unable to meet the boy's direct gaze, and immediately knew where she was.

Just below her, beyond the bushes, she could see the canal and the tow-path. She knew these two sheds. You could see their roofs just before you got to Buxton Tunnel. She'd never realized they were in Buxton House garden before. But how did that help? She couldn't just break down the window, dive into the canal and escape from this extraordinary boy. She wished his dad had come out and told her off. That would have been normal and ordinary. Sitting here with him was weird.

'So, who are you?' he asked, cheerfully. 'No, don't tell me. I bet you're Flora that lives on the *Thorpe Cloud*.'

'How do you…?' Flora was too startled to finish.

'I know 'cos I ask people. It's easy. I know the names of all the people who live along this stretch of the canal. I haven't met them all yet, but I will.'

Flora was sure he would. She thought he'd get on well with Joss. He was so confident.

'So why were you watching Dad? Why didn't you just knock on the door?' Flora shifted uncomfortably on her chair. She couldn't possibly explain. But the boy wasn't worried. 'OK, forget I asked, then,' he said. 'It doesn't really matter anyway.'

Flora blinked at him. She could think of nothing whatsoever to say. Everything the boy said was a surprise. He looked at her, anxious again. 'I say, are you all right?' he asked. 'You didn't bash your head or something, did you?'

Flora tried very hard to pull herself together. 'No, I'm fine,' she said, firmly. 'But who *are* you?'

The boy looked at her in surprise. 'Gosh, didn't I say?

19

I'm Tan. Well, Nathaniel really, but everyone calls me Tan.'

'Tan! Tan! Come on, please. It's teatime!' It was the pancake man calling.

'You see?' said Tan, with a grin. 'Come on, then. D'you like pancakes? Oh, I forgot. You didn't want Dad to see you—you never told me why.'

He paused and looked at Flora hopefully.

So he *did* want to know.

'I... I... I don't know really,' she stammered nervously, wishing Buxton House had never existed. 'I was just looking around. I thought he might be cross.'

'Dad? Not on your life. Come and meet him.'

'No, I've got to get back,' said Flora, grasping her chance for escape before Tan swept her into the house. 'I only said I was going for a quick walk.'

'Well, come round tomorrow after school then. What time do you finish?'

'Half past three,' said Flora, automatically. 'But I won't get here till about four because of the bus.' She shook herself. What was she saying? She wasn't coming here again tomorrow, was she? Was she?

'Stay for tea then,' said Tan. 'I'll be waiting for you at four.'

'But won't I see you at school?' asked Flora, hesitantly.

'No way,' said Tan, with a chuckle. 'I don't go.'

3

Flora didn't sleep well that night. Tan didn't go to school. *Tan didn't go to school.* For hours she lay awake, weighing up this completely new idea. Oh, she'd dreamed of governesses, of course, but had never seriously believed they still existed, even for child stars. Tan must have one. What other solution could there be? She knew that if you were ill and off school for months there were special teachers who would come to your house, but there didn't seem to be anything wrong with Tan. Perhaps he just meant that he didn't go to school right now because of moving house. Yes, that must be it. Because everyone in Britain had to go to school. Didn't they?

Finally she fell into an uneasy sleep, her mind set on one thing. She would go tomorrow. She would do as he'd told her and meet him by the gate—and she wouldn't leave until she'd found out exactly what he had meant.

It was a hard job getting up in the morning but Flora felt strangely excited. Joss was on a school trip that day and had set off early, so Flora had no one to talk to at the bus-stop. For once she was quite glad. Some strange urge made her want to keep Tan to herself. It was odd; she always told Joss everything. And she wasn't even sure she liked Tan yet.

The day passed surprisingly quickly. Normally, every minute in school seemed an eternity. Today her mind was somewhere else and her teachers found her even more difficult to teach than usual.

She leaped off the school bus excitedly at the end of the day and ran along the tow-path to the *Thorpe Cloud*, only to find that Libby wasn't there. Painfully, she wrote a note in her awkward handwriting and then skipped off to meet Tan. Libby wouldn't mind her going to Tan's house, would she? It wasn't as if she was going past Buxton Tunnel.

She arrived breathless and hot. Tan was hanging upside-down on the gate.

'You're early,' he said, cheerfully.

'You said you didn't go to school,' Flora panted, before she lost her nerve. 'What did you mean?'

'Just that I don't,' Tan replied, casually, without bothering to change his position. 'Why?'

'But you can't!' said Flora, flustered. 'There are laws about it. Everyone in this country has to go to school.'

'Wrong!' said Tan, looking pleased with himself. 'Everyone has to be *educated*. No one has to go to school.'

'So have you got a governess or something?' demanded Flora. 'How do you get educated without going to school? Have you got a tutor? What do you have to do?'

Tan swung upright. 'Hang on a minute. What's bugging you? You look like you're going to explode.'

'I will if you don't tell me what you mean,' shouted Flora, and surprised herself by stamping her foot in the dirt. 'What d'you mean, you don't go to school? I don't understand! What d'you mean? What d'you mean? What

22

d'you mean?' And, to her great shame, she burst into tears of fury and frustration.

Tan looked horrified. 'Hey, I'm sorry,' he said. 'I didn't know it would upset you so much. I'm just educated at home, that's all. It's not that unusual. My dad teaches me some of the time and a lot of the time I just get on with the things I'm interested in. That's all, really. It's not such a big deal.'

Flora gulped frantically and wiped her eyes on her sleeve. 'It is to me,' she wailed. 'I'd do anything to stop having to go.'

'Oh,' said Tan. 'Why?'

'Because I hate it.' Flora looked very hard at the boats in the distance. She was determined not to cry again.

'Well, I'd hate it too, I think,' said Tan. 'Except for having loads of kids to play with. But why do you hate it so much?'

Flora took a deep breath and let rip. No one had ever asked her that before; they were all too busy trying to tell her how important it was. 'I hate it all,' she said in a low, hard voice. 'Everything. It's too hot and big and noisy and everyone treats me like I'm thick. And I *feel* thick at school. The other kids tease me 'cos I live on a boat. You always have to do what the teachers say, even if you think it's really stupid and if you ever do get to do anything you like, the bell goes and it's time for play-time or PE or assembly or something else really boring. It's not like I don't want to learn, but the teachers never have enough time to explain anything properly and then I do it all wrong and I get all stressed out and I get a headache or my eczema goes mad and I just hate it! I hate it! I hate it!'

'Crikey!' said Tan, winded by her fury.

Flora slowly unclenched her fists. 'Sorry,' she said, defiantly.

'Tell you what, ' said Tan, just a little nervously. 'Why don't we go and see what's for tea?'

A wonderful aroma of baking drifted out of the kitchen door and Flora suddenly realized she was so hungry that her legs were shaking. She'd been too worked up to make much of her lunch and the scene with Tan had used up the last of her energy. If she didn't eat soon, she knew exactly what would happen. She'd get a migraine. Then she'd be in bed for hours and hours, blinded with pain, and too sick to eat or move. The curtains at the portholes would be shut tight as light would be unbearable. She would live in a strange twilight world of pain and loneliness and exhaustion. Even the gentle rhythm of the water lapping against the boat would feel like hammers beating at her brain and she would lie very still, praying that a motor cruiser wouldn't go by. Once Joss' family had had a party and she had thought that she would die of the pain. Libby now told them when Flora was ill, so she only had to suffer the guilt of being a nuisance. And at least it meant some time off school.

But this time Flora didn't want to be ill. Life had suddenly become exciting. Flora wanted to know more about this strange boy who didn't go to school and his pancake-making dad. She must ask for some food even though there was nothing on the table yet. She must. Quickly. Before it was too late and the migraine struck.

But she couldn't do it. She simply couldn't bring herself to demand food the moment she was over the threshold. Joss would have done it for her. But Flora was on her own and shyness clamped her mouth.

Perhaps she would be all right. There was no knowing with migraines.

'This is Flora, Dad,' said Tan, bouncing into the kitchen. 'Come on, don't just stand in the doorway, Flora. Come right in!'

'Give her time, Tan,' said the pancake man, genially. 'You'll frighten her to death.'

He wiped his hands on his apron and held one out. 'Sorry about the flour,' he said with a friendly smile. 'I'm David. I hope you like scones. I'm doing loads. And there's a big hotpot in the Aga too. Should be ready in about an hour.'

Flora grasped the large, flour-smeared hand. *Now's your chance*, a voice in her head whispered urgently. *Ask for a scone. Or some bread. Quick!*

'Pleased to meet you,' Flora muttered, shyly. 'Thank you for letting me come for tea.'

Flora decided very quickly that she had never met anyone quite so easy to talk to as Tan's dad. He had a kind, lined face which never fell into that glazed, far-away look that adults have when they're trying to be polite but aren't listening to a word you're saying. And she found she was quickly getting used to Tan. He was only odd in that he said exactly what he thought and asked exactly what he wanted to know. Between the two of them, they soon had almost her entire life history. But she didn't tell them about the migraines. She was too conscious of the time-bomb ticking away inside her. Already the bright evening light was beginning to make her wince. Tea was delicious when it came and Flora ate ravenously, hoping against hope that she hadn't left it too late. Already glowing white zig-zags had begun to dart across her vision, but perhaps if she ignored them they would go away and she'd get home before the explosion.

Suddenly she noticed the kitchen clock.

'Oh no!' she gasped. 'Ten to seven! Is that the right time? My mum always wants me home by seven!'

She stood up hurriedly and that was when the bomb went off.

'Oh no!' she gasped again, but this time she clutched the side of her head and grabbed at the table to steady herself.

'What is it?' Tan and his dad both leaped to their feet.

'I'm sorry, I don't feel very well,' mumbled Flora and sat down. The pain had hit with the suddenness of a tornado but she was safe from the sickness for a while. 'I need to go home,' she said, every word an effort. Hopelessly, she sank her head onto her arms. 'I'm sorry,' she said, thickly.

Tan's dad sprang round the table and lifted her head gently. All Flora's colour had gone, except that her lips were a startling pink.

'What is it, Dad?' demanded Tan, urgently. 'Shall I call an ambulance?'

'No, I know what it is,' he said quietly, 'though I didn't know kids got it. It's migraine. That's it, isn't it, Flora? Your mum used to get them, Tan.'

Flora nodded miserably. 'I'm sorry,' she whispered.

Tan's dad put his arm round her. He spoke very quietly. 'It's all right, Flora. It isn't your fault. Now we've just got to get you home, OK?'

He scooped up Flora's limp little body. 'Come on, Tan,' he said. 'Grab the car keys. We'll go round by road.'

Then, walking with the delicacy of a pedigree cat, he carried Flora out of the house.

It was only a matter of minutes before they had drawn up in the village and were all hurrying along the short stretch of the tow-path to the *Thorpe Cloud*, Tan's dad carrying Flora as protectively as possible.

'Run ahead and tell her mum,' he told Tan, who shot off immediately, but seconds later was back.

'She's not in,' he said, excitedly, 'but she can't have gone far. The door's not locked.'

Flora groaned softly and a silent tear rolled down her face.

'It's all right,' Tan's dad said softly. 'We'll look after you, Flora.'

'Gone looking for me,' Flora mumbled, each word painfully slow. 'Cross with me.'

'Don't worry,' said Tan, his bright face clouded with concern. 'Dad'll explain.'

His father edged his way up the gangplank and gently kicked open the door. Flora's bunk was easy to spot. She had a Winnie-the-Pooh duvet cover. He lay her down gently.

'D'you take any medicine for this?' he asked.

'Cupboard over sink,' Flora whispered and clung to Tan's dad's sleeve. 'Don't leave me.'

'We won't, I promise. I'll just get something cold to put on your head. Tan, find that medicine quickly.'

'Need bowl,' gasped Flora, and by some miracle he heard what she said and found one before she was violently sick.

'Sorry,' she whispered and collapsed back on her pillow, exhausted, at which very moment the door burst open and in stormed Libby, red in the face, panting and clearly in an extremely bad mood.

'What...?' she exclaimed, brought up short by the

sight of Tan rummaging in her medicine cupboard. 'Who the…? What are you doing on my boat? And where's Flora?'

Tan's dad stepped into the kitchen area.

'I'm terrribly sorry, Mrs…'

'Ms Adams,' snapped Libby. 'Can I please have some sort of explanation, or shall I call the police?'

From her bunk, Flora groaned.

'Flora!' Libby pushed Tan aside. 'What have they done to you?'

But his father was ahead of her and was already busy with the bowl.

'Migraine,' he said, shortly. 'It came on just after tea, so we brought Flora home but you weren't here.' He gave her an accusing look.

Libby's face was equally steely. 'I went to meet her. When she hadn't got back by quarter to seven, I decided to walk along to Buxton House. It was getting rather late.' Libby said this with emphasis, as if it was his fault. 'And when I got to your house—I presume you are the owner of Buxton House?—there was no one there!'

'I'm sorry,' said Tan's dad, his face softening slightly. 'You must have just missed us. We came round by the road. I wanted to get Flora home as quickly as possible. I'm David Blake.'

Libby drew herself up in a dignified manner. 'I apologize if I was somewhat abrupt. You've obviously been very kind,' she said, stiffly. 'Flora has been very naughty, though. She didn't ask me if she could go to tea with you. I just found this note when I got home.' She stopped to fish out a crumpled piece of paper from the pocket of her jeans and tossed it onto David's lap. 'I've never even met you before. I know hardly anything

28

about you. Imagine how I felt when I got to your house and no one was there. I didn't know what to do. I...' Here Libby stopped, rubbed her eyes vainly and then, to David's horror and Tan's amazement, she burst into tears.

'Oh crikey,' said Tan.

4

Flora opened her eyes. It didn't hurt. She raised herself tentatively on one elbow. OK so far. She would have to go to the loo. The acid test. Carefully she sat up and swung her legs round. It was going to be all right. She felt dull and heavy and fragile but the pain and the nausea had gone. Libby would expect her to go to school.

Libby had already started working when Flora was ready for breakfast, so it was a surprise when she spoke.

'Are you sure you're all right to get up, Flora? You look very pale.'

'I'm OK,' said Flora, dully. 'I had a whole day in bed yesterday. And you've got your work to do.'

Libby leaned back on her chair and drummed her fingers on the table restlessly.

'I've been talking to David,' she said.

'David?' Flora looked blank.

'You know, Tan's dad. Buxton House. The bloke who held the bowl while you were sick.'

'Oh, him. Why've you been talking to him?'

'Because I was worried about you, twitface, and he was there. He brought you home, remember?'

'Well, only sort of,' said Flora.

'Right. Well, I have to admit I hadn't really realized how bad these migraines of yours are. To be honest, I thought you were making a bit of a fuss and using them as an excuse to stay off school.'

Flora said nothing. She could think of better ways of getting out of school, but Libby didn't need to know that.

'Well, David's wife used to have them so he knows a lot about them. He thinks there are things we can do to help and that when you do have an attack, I shouldn't rush you back to school as soon as you can stand up. He says that might be making you worse.'

Flora felt slightly dizzy. It was as if something on wings was taking off inside her head. Surely Libby wasn't going to suggest another day off school? She'd already had one.

'But what about your work?' she stammered. 'Won't I get in the way?'

'David says you can spend the day with him and Tan, if you like. You'll have to occupy yourself quietly or rest in the morning because they'll both be working, but in the afternoon you could do some pottery or painting or baking or something. Would you like that?'

Flora's eyes were round with wonder.

'But you hardly know them,' she objected. 'And I thought you didn't like Tan's dad.'

'What on earth made you think that?' asked Libby, somewhat snappishly, her fingers drumming the table again.

'I don't know.' Flora felt confused. She couldn't remember much about what had happened after Tan's dad had brought her home; she just had this feeling that Libby had been very cross about something. It was all very odd. Libby had waited a whole year before she had felt she knew Zilla and Reuben well enough to

31

leave Flora with them.

'Well?' said Libby, impatiently. 'What d'you think? Would you like to spend the day with David and Tan?'

'Oh yes!' agreed Flora quickly, before this freak moment passed and Libby changed her mind. 'Of course I would. It'd make me feel much better than going to school.'

'Well, that's settled then. Hurry up and eat your breakfast. David said they'd come and get you at about half past eight.'

Flora was just starting on her second bowl of cereal— she hadn't eaten for a whole day—when Joss arrived.

'Hi, Flora,' she beamed. 'I thought you must be better by now, what with Libby going out last night and everything. Hurry up and finish your breakfast or we'll miss the bus.'

Libby had gone out last night? Odd. She almost never went out—and to go when Flora was ill was unheard of. But Flora's mind was too busy with other things to dwell on it for long. 'I'm not coming,' she said through a mouthful of Rice Krispies. She was trying not to grin too broadly; she didn't want Libby to know how much she hated school.

'Not coming?' Joss was taken aback. 'Are you still poorly, then?'

'I've decided she ought to take things more slowly when she's had one of her migraines,' cut in Libby, 'so she's going to have another day off.'

'Oh,' said Joss. She looked as if she was about to say something else, but must have changed her mind. She turned to go. 'Bye, then, Flora,' she said. 'I'll see you this evening, OK? Glad you're getting better.'

Joss was just about to mount the steps out of the

cabin when the door burst open and Tan nearly fell down them.

'Is Flora ready?' he demanded. 'Dad's waiting with the car.'

'Is he?' Libby pushed her work aside. 'I'll just nip along and have a word with him, then. Hurry up, Flora.'

There was an awkward silence when she'd gone, but Tan soon broke it.

'Hi, I'm Tan,' he said. 'You must be Joss from next door.'

Joss barely nodded. 'What's going on, Flora?' she demanded. She seemed annoyed for some reason which Flora didn't understand. 'Why are you going off with him if you're too poorly to come to school?'

Flora shrugged helplessly. 'I don't really know,' she said. 'Mum just thinks I ought to have a quiet day and Tan's dad said he would look after me 'cos she's got her work to do.'

'Oh well,' said Joss, dismissively. 'It's none of my business, I suppose. Better go or I'll miss the bus.' And with that, she went.

'Well, she doesn't seem very friendly,' said Tan. 'Is she always like that?'

'Like what?' said Flora. 'I don't know what you mean.'

'Bossy.'

Flora giggled, despite still feeling rough. 'That's good, you calling Joss bossy. *You're* the bossiest person I've ever met.'

'I am not.'

'Oh yes you are.'

'Am not.'

'Are.'

'Oh, shut up and finish your breakfast. Dad's waiting.'

33

'See! See what I mean?' Flora grinned. She had never come round from a migraine and felt so happy.

Flora had a lovely day. She hadn't found the courage before to ask what Tan's dad did for a living and was thrilled to discover that he was an artist and had illustrated some of her favourite picture-books. She spent the morning happily browsing through some of his folders of work and then curled up asleep on a big, battered sofa at the side of his studio. Tan was working on a project about the Tudors and spent a large part of the time constructing a life-size model of an Elizabethan man. He had made the body out of old clothes stuffed with newspaper and was now adding the detail.

'Did all the blokes have these short, fat pants, d'you think?' he asked Flora.

'I haven't a clue,' she replied. She vaguely remembered having done the Tudors at school but she was learning more about them watching Tan this morning than she had ever done then.

After lunch Tan's dad asked her if she'd like to have a go with some clay. 'Tan's mum was a potter,' he said, 'and we've still got all her stuff—but you'll have to wait a while before we can fire anything. I haven't got the kiln installed yet.'

'What happened to your mum?' asked Flora, in a small voice, when she and Tan were busy with the clay, which seemed to have the effect of shutting his mouth.

'Fell off a mountain,' said Tan, curtly.

'Oh. Was she a rock-climber then?'

'No. Just going for a walk with Dad. They liked hiking.'

'Was it long ago?'

34

'I was a baby. I was in one of those backpack things on Dad.'

Flora fell silent, imagining the scene. She conjured up a wild mountain ridge with David and a young, pretty woman walking one behind the other. The woman turned, laughter in her face, to talk to her husband and her baby, perched chortling on his dad's back. A freak gust of wind, she slipped and... it was too horrible to go on.

Without realizing it, she had stopped rolling the sausage she needed for her coil pot. Her eyes were glazed and her shoulders tense.

'Flora? You all right?' said Tan.

Flora shook herself. 'I was just thinking about it. How can your dad bear it? How can he be so... well, nice?'

Tan shrugged. 'I'm not sure. He believes God has a plan. He's like that.'

'It doesn't sound like a very good one,' said Flora.

Tan shrugged again. 'Well, it keeps Dad happy, anyway.'

David didn't take Flora home until after tea and, even more surprisingly, until he'd made her have a long soak in the huge bath.

'It'll make you relax,' he said, 'and get rid of all that clay you've got lurking under your fingernails!'

Flora sank back into the water blissfully. A bath was the sort of luxury she could only indulge in when she and Libby visited relatives. And this bath was huge! The surroundings weren't very luxurious—bare boards and peeling paintwork—but Flora didn't care. She'd been feeling better all day and as the hot water lapped round her neck, she could feel it easing away the last of the groggy, tight feeling.

David lent her a pair of Tan's pyjamas to wear under her sweatshirt.

'Then you can go straight to bed when you get home,' he said.

It was lovely to be driven home feeling so clean and cosy and relaxed.

'Like the outfit, Flora,' called Joss, spotting them from where she was lounging on the grass by the towpath. For some reason it didn't sound entirely friendly, but Flora was too happy to worry about it straightaway.

'You're back late,' said Joss when they were level with her.

'Sorry,' said Flora, a little knot of worry tying itself inside her. Joss seemed unaccountably cross again.

'I wanted to talk to you,' she said.

'I'm sorry,' said David. 'Were you expecting her? I thought a nice, long bath would do her good.'

Joss looked slightly envious. 'Oh, that's OK. It didn't really matter.'

But Flora had this funny feeling that for some reason it did.

Flora couldn't get to sleep. She had a lot to think about. She had just spent a day of quiet bliss and something inside her had changed for ever. So school wasn't a 'have to'. All right then, she wasn't going to. She wasn't going to waste her life being miserable when there were days of peace and happiness just waiting to be enjoyed. It wasn't that she didn't want an education—but she had learned more in one day at Tan's house than she had in months at school. It had fascinated her to watch David at work and she longed to have a go herself. Painting at school meant struggling with worn-out, abused brushes and foul-smelling, gunged-up powder paint which irritated her skin, worlds apart from the beauty and order of David's studio. And pottery meant hurried sessions with a visiting potter whose one concern seemed to be that you didn't use too much clay. At Tan's house she had sat in the cool of the studio for the whole afternoon, perfecting silky smooth coil after silky smooth coil and moulding her pot higher and higher and higher. She hadn't given her eczema a thought and her migraine had only got better.

There was no point in broaching the subject with Libby. An occasional day at Tan's to recover after a migraine was all that Libby would allow. Flora didn't need to ask; she just knew. Libby believed in school. For her, school had meant the qualifications that none of the rest of her family had. It had led to university and freedom—for a while at least. Then Flora had come along. And now Libby had her work. There was no way she could consider educating Flora at home.

It was Saturday tomorrow. Flora had two whole days to sort out a plan. Two whole days to persuade Tan to help her. With that reassuring thought firmly fixed in her mind, Flora finally fell asleep.

5

It was nearly eleven o'clock when Flora awoke the following morning. She stretched herself happily, hugging her new-found knowledge to herself. No one had to go to school in Britain. And she wasn't going to go. She was going to find a way out.

Normally she would have been annoyed to have wasted some precious hours of the weekend, but now everything was different. She strolled through to the living area in her pyjamas and started to make some toast.

Libby looked up from her typewriter.

'Feeling better? Your colour's come back, thank goodness.'

'I'm fine,' said Flora, cheerfully. 'Want some coffee?'

'No, don't worry. Just hurry and get yourself something. If you're feeling well enough, we're off for a picnic with David and Tan.'

'What, now?' said Flora, her heart soaring. Now she wouldn't need to find an excuse to go and see Tan. It ought to be easy to find a chance to talk to him privately while they were out. It was all rather astonishing though. For as long as Flora could remember, Libby had been a loner. She kept herself to herself and it took her a long time to make friends. That was one reason she liked living on the canal.

'Canal people accept you as you are,' she often said. 'They're not for ever asking nosy questions.'

So this sudden friendliness with Tan and David was a bit of a shock—but then they were rather hard to resist. Tan, especially, was one of those people who didn't take no for an answer.

Flora hurriedly got herself ready and helped Libby to pack a picnic. To her amazement, Libby produced a tray of marshmallow krispie cake and packed it in the bag.

'Have you sold a story or something?' Flora demanded. 'I thought we only had that for birthdays!'

Libby blushed. 'I thought I should make a bit of an effort since they've been so kind and helpful,' she explained.

'Oh,' said Flora and wondered if she ought to have migraines more often.

They'd just finished clearing away when Tan arrived, breathless and bossy as usual.

'Come on,' he said. 'Dad's waiting with the car. I'll carry that cake. Don't suppose you've got a kite?'

Libby burst out laughing. 'Where would we keep one?' she said, glancing round their cramped quarters.

'Oh well. You can borrow one of ours. Dad makes them. Come on, then.'

Obediently, they followed Tan onto the tow-path, only to find Joss just about to come aboard.

'We must stop meeting like this,' said Tan, cheerily. Joss glowered at him.

'You're not off again are you, Flora?' she said, grumpily. 'I wanted to talk to you. I told you last night.'

'I'm really sorry,' said Flora, embarrassed. 'I only just got up and we're off for a picnic. I promise I'll be here this evening. I will, won't I, Mum?'

'Oh, I should think so,' said Libby, easily. 'But we'd better get going now. OK, Joss?'

Flora allowed herself to be hurried along, but her mood wasn't as buoyant as it had been. Something was wrong. Joss would never normally make a fuss about not being able to have a chat. Flora tried to dwell on the picnic and kite flying. She didn't want to think about lovely, colourful, friendly Joss left looking rather forlorn on the tow-path.

Flora had known where they were going the minute kites had been mentioned. There was only one place you flew kites around here and that was on a small out-crop of hills, the only really high ground for miles around. An old Armada beacon stood there and the remains of old quarry workings made fantastic places to scramble and play kick-the-can. They hadn't been very often—only when piles of Libby's relatives descended and there wasn't enough room on the boat. And they'd never flown kites.

'You wait till you see Dad's kites,' said Tan, excitedly, as they drove along. 'He painted them himself. And they fly brilliantly.'

Is there anything David can't do? thought Flora. Pancake man, painter man, kite man. It was a good job he was also such a nice man or it would be enough to make you sick.

The kites were splendid, of course. One was a snake, one was a rooster and one was a tiger.

'He made them when I was doing a project on China,' Tan explained as they watched David make the snake soar into the air. 'Because of the years we were born—you know, the Chinese animal years. I was born in the year of the tiger, Mum was the year of the rooster and Dad the year of the snake.'

'Oh, I see,' said Flora, not seeing at all. There was such a lot she didn't know. And she certainly didn't know how Tan could bear to talk about his mother so casually. But then, he would hardly remember her. It made Flora want to cry. She couldn't remember her dad at all, of course, but that was different. Worse or better she couldn't decide, but she was so used to knowing that he hadn't wanted anything to do with her that it never occurred to her to cry about it.

'Come on,' said Tan. 'Let's get my kite up. Once you know what you're doing, I'll get Rooster up too and you can have Tiger, OK?'

'What about your dad and my mum?'

'Oh, they'll be all right,' Tan shrugged. 'Look.'

Sure enough, they were happily occupied. David was standing behind Libby, his hands guiding hers, rescuing the snake kite when it might have come crashing down.

Perhaps now was the time to talk to Tan about her plans? thought Flora. *Now that the grown-ups were out of the way?* But suddenly she felt nervous. Her plans were so outrageous really. And she'd known Tan for less than a week. The kites were beckoning. She longed to have Tiger dancing at the end of his line for herself. Her plans could wait. She would find the right moment later.

But she never did. It was too intoxicating, once she'd got the knack, racing Tiger through the sky and frantically battling to save him from each undignified death. And when he did come crashing down, she simply had to get him aloft again. *Just one more time,* she kept saying to herself. *Just one more time.*

When they finally stopped for a very late lunch, Flora

could have dragged Tan off for a chat. 'Exploring' would have been a good excuse. But Flora was shy. What if he laughed at her idea? What if he thought she was silly? Everything she knew about him so far told her that he wouldn't, but she had known him such a short time! The words wouldn't come.

After lunch they clambered on the rocks, played Frisbee in the open spaces and then had a glorious game of kick-the-can until they were too exhausted to play any more.

'Come back and eat with us,' said David as they packed all their things away. 'And use our bath, if you like. You don't want to stiffen up after all that exercise.'

For a moment Flora was sure Libby was going to agree. It was the obvious end to a perfect day. But then Libby's face changed slightly. It seemed to stiffen up.

'That's really kind,' she said, politely, 'but I think we should be getting back now. We don't want to trespass on your hospitality too much and we do have a perfectly reasonable shower, you know.'

'As you like,' said David, cordially, but he seemed more distant somehow. Flora was puzzled and then remembered that she had thought at first that they didn't like one another. She was also a bit cross. She would have loved another soak in David's wonderful, deep bath.

Everyone was rather quiet on the way home, including Tan. Flora found herself nodding sleepily, despite her lie-in that morning. It was a wrench to get herself out of the car and walk the short distance along the tow-path to the *Thorpe Cloud*. She was just thinking how nice it would be to have a cup of tea and a shower when Libby spoke.

'Hadn't you better go and see Joss now, before we eat? She seemed pretty desperate to speak to you and I think they'll be out later, playing at a barn dance.'

Flora groaned. 'Oh, I suppose so,' she said and then felt guilty. How had things changed so fast? Only on Monday Flora would have leaped at the chance of a chat with Joss and now here she was, complaining because she had something important to tell her. It was very disloyal. Tan was nice but there was no way he could replace Joss. Was there?

Quickly Flora tapped on the door of Joss' boat and was let in by a welcoming Zilla.

'Flora, pet, are you better now?' she demanded and grabbed Flora by the shoulders to inspect her closely. 'Hmm. Much better, by the look of things. You were a poorly girl last night. You didn't even notice it was me looking after you and not your mum.'

'Didn't I? Did you?' said Flora, confused. Of course! Joss had said something about Libby going out and Flora had forgotten all about it. But before she had a chance to ask where Libby had been, Zilla was hurrying her through to see Joss.

'Now you go and have a nice chat with Joscelyn, all right? She's been moping around all day about something or other but I'm blowed if I can get her to tell me what it's all about. See if you can do any better.'

The *Argo* was a longer boat than the *Thorpe Cloud* and moored alongside it was a second boat called a butty boat, so Joss' family had over twice as much space as Libby and Flora. Now that the older children had moved out Joss had her own cabin, not just a bunk at the side of some corridor space like Flora. It fascinated Flora. Joss had decked it out like the inside of a tent in some exotic bazaar, draping the walls and windows in flamboyant cloths and hanging mobiles and wind chimes from the eaves. Every available ledge was crowded with a clutter of ornaments and candle-holders and the air was always thick with the scent of perfumed wax. Flora knew that she would never have been able to sleep in there, what with the smell and the gentle jingling of the chimes, but it suited Joss.

This evening, however, there were no candles lit and Flora could barely make out Joss, half-buried in the multi-coloured cushions which littered her bed.

'Hi,' said Flora, a bit nervously. 'I'm sorry we were rushing off earlier.'

'It's OK,' Joss grunted. 'Did you have a nice time?'

'Great, thanks,' said Flora but decided Joss wouldn't want to know just how great. She sat down uneasily on a large cushion which half-filled the floor space and wondered what to say. This was all most unlike Joss.

'Is there something the matter, Joss?' she said at last in a small voice. 'You don't seem very well.'

'I heard them talking,' said Joss, gruffly, and to Flora's horror she sounded very close to tears.

'Who? What about?' she asked, anxiously. It all seemed so strange and serious. Flora felt she was the last person Joss ought to be talking to.

'Zilla and Reuben. They thought I was asleep. The boat yard where Dad works is going to close. The council want to build a new canalside shopping centre in town and jazz it up—try to pretend it's Venice or somewhere—so there won't be room for a dirty old boat yard.'

'Oh,' said Flora. She wasn't really sure what else to say.

'But don't you see? If the boat yard closes, we'll have to move on. Oh, the music brings in some money and so does Mum's work, but it's Dad's job which brings in the most regularly.'

Flora felt a cold pebble of panic trickle down her insides. Joss was going to go? What would she do without her? The horror of the idea drove all thoughts of Tan and David from her mind.

'But I thought boat people liked to move on,' she blustered. 'Not pretend boat people like me and Mum, but proper ones like you.' Joss must never know how desperately she needed her. She would think she was a complete wimp.

'Well, I don't,' said Joss, stubbornly. 'I like it here and I want to stay. And it's a really good job Dad's got—it'd be impossible to find another one like that. And Mum's all sorted, just doing a bit part-time at the Alternative Health Centre. They don't really want to move on either. They're getting too old.'

'They're not old,' said Flora, shocked. 'You're only eleven.'

'They're both over fifty. My eldest sister is twenty-eight, remember.'

Flora had forgotten—or at least, she had never given it much thought. To her, grown-ups were grown-ups.

'Well,' she said brightly, hoping that Joss wouldn't notice that her hands were trembling, 'it's quite a good time to move in a way, what with changing schools and everything.'

'Oh, thank you,' said Joss furiously, suddenly sitting bolt upright on the bed. 'Boat people like moving on! I'm changing schools anyway! And I thought you were my friend. I've been waiting and waiting to tell you

45

about it and that's all I get. You sound like you don't care at all whether I go or stay! And after all those notes I've written for you too!'

'I didn't mean... I was just trying...' Too late, Flora realized the huge blunder she had made.

'Oh, don't bother!' stormed Joss. 'It's quite obvious what you meant. You've taken up with that mouthy prat Tan and you don't care about me any more. Well, you're welcome to him. I don't know why I ever bothered with a scabby little drip like you!'

Flora's head reeled. What had she done? Why on earth had she said that about changing schools? Of course it was tactless. And what had Joss said about Tan? She couldn't really be jealous? Could she? What had she said? It was all mixed up in Flora's head now. She just knew she had made Joss very, very angry, Joss who had always been so kind to her...

A SCABBY LITTLE DRIP!!!

No! So that was what Joss really thought! How two-faced could you get? Well, Flora wasn't taking that. No way. A week ago she might have but, like a sudden beam of light through the fog in her brain, she remembered Tan and David. She didn't have to depend on Joss. Other people liked her too. She wasn't going to stand around and be insulted. A scabby little drip, was she?

Quick as a flash, Flora reached out and slapped Joss hard across the face. Stunned, Joss fell back on her bed. Then, with a roar of fury, she launched herself across the cabin, at which point Zilla opened the door.

'Joscelyn! Flora!' she said, her face a mask of horror. 'What *is* going on?'

'I'm just going,' said Flora, hurriedly and tried to squeeze past Zilla's bulky form.

'Wimp,' seethed Joss. 'That's right, just walk away when the going gets tough. Well, smarty-pants, you might find you're moving on too, you know. You might find you're moving *in* with your precious Tan and David. 'Cos you know where Libby went last night when you were ill, don't you? Down to Buxton House to see darling Dave. I wonder if you'll like them so much when you have to live with them all the time, huh?'

Tears were pouring down Flora's cheeks now and she had to wipe them on her sleeve to speak, but there was real rage in her voice.

'I don't believe you, Joscelyn Robinson,' she said. 'You're making it up. And I'll never bother to speak to you again! Never, ever, ever, not as long as I live. I can manage without you, thanks very much. Just you wait and see.'

6

Flora stood on the tow-path outside the *Argo*, trembling. She couldn't let Libby see her like this. She couldn't tell her what had happened or what Joss had said, though she was bound to find out some part of it before long. She would go for a quick walk; the breeze would cool her hot cheeks and soothe her head, which was aching again.

She hurried along the tow-path, unconsciously distancing herself as far as possible from Joss. Within minutes she could see Buxton House. Her first instinct was to run and find David and tell him everything. He would calm her down and give her something to eat; he might even let her have a bath and drive her home, all warm and sleepy and ready for bed.

But no. She couldn't do that. It wasn't as simple as that any more. Everything had changed. David was part of the row.

What had Joss said? Flora's brain was a confused fug of things she wished hadn't been voiced. Resolutely, she stood stock-still and went over it.

'...'cos you know where Libby went last night when you were ill, don't you? Down to Buxton House to see darling Dave. I wonder if you'll like them so much when you have to live with them all the time?'

It couldn't be like that! It just couldn't. Libby hardly

knew David. They had only just met. Yes, they seemed very friendly most of the time, but what about that funny bit when David had suggested they went back to Buxton House and Libby had behaved almost as if he was a complete stranger? No, Joss must be wrong, she must be. David and Tan were great and Flora really liked them, but they had to stay safely at Buxton House, whilst she and Libby stayed on the *Thorpe Cloud*. Things had to stay the same—just nicer.

Flora turned on her heel and started for home. She couldn't run to David. Not now. Not any more.

And then she remembered. Things had been going to change. She had been going to change them herself. She had had plans. Plans to persuade Tan to ask his dad if she could come and have lessons at Buxton House— without Libby ever knowing. She had worked it all out. David would write a letter saying that the *Thorpe Cloud* was moving on and that Flora would therefore be leaving the school. Then Flora would leave home each morning as normal but instead of getting the bus she would go round by road to Buxton House. And Joss would be in on the plot and would cover for her.

Not any more.

Flora began to run. She had to get back to her little space on the *Thorpe Cloud* and bury her head in her pillow before she began to cry again. Libby would be expecting her back soon anyway.

In a matter of moments Flora was mounting the gangplank to the *Thorpe Cloud*. Then she stopped. Voices. Through the closed door, Flora could hear them perfectly clearly: Libby's sharp and surprised, Zilla's all apology and concern.

'I should have talked it all through with her properly

as soon as we knew,' Zilla was saying, guiltily. 'If I'd done that there would never have been all this trouble with Flora. Joss obviously needed someone to talk to and poor little Flora just said all the wrong things. It wasn't her fault, poor little mite.'

Flora winced. These days she was feeling a bit too old for Zilla's rather sugary sympathy.

'There was no excuse for hitting Joss, though,' said Libby. 'I…'

Flora decided she had heard enough. She should have realized that Zilla would be straight over to see Libby. There was only one place to go. Back down the tow-path.

She ran quickly, half-blinded by tears, her breath coming in gasps. What she would do when she reached Buxton House again, she didn't know. She just had to get away.

She stopped. It was impossible to run any further without blowing her nose and she had to root through her pockets before she found a very tired ball of tissue. She walked on slowly. She had a stitch and her legs ached. What was she to do?

The gate of Buxton House. Decision time. Flora stood with her hand on the latch, mentally tossing a coin. Here, at least, she could hide in Tan's den for a while and have a proper cry. She pushed open the gate. It would be OK; Tan would probably be having tea.

He wasn't. He was coming up the path from his shed, straight towards Flora. Too late she spotted him and tried to jump aside into the bushes.

'Flora! What are you doing here?' he demanded. 'You nearly frightened me to death, hopping about like that!'

'Oh, nothing,' Flora protested, backing away hurriedly.

'It doesn't matter. I'm on my way home.'

Tan was too quick for her.

'Just a minute,' he said, darting forward and grabbing her wrist. 'You've been crying. Something's wrong. Tell me what it is.'

'Let go, Tan. You're hurting my wrist. It's nothing. Honestly.'

'But why are you here? Why were you coming to the den? I don't get it, Flora.'

'You don't have to. Just let me go. Libby'll go mad if I'm late back. Please, Tan. Let me go. Please.' She was gabbling at him in her anxiety to get away.

'I'm coming with you, then,' said Tan. 'You're too upset to go home on your own.'

'I'm not upset,' retorted Flora, suddenly angry. He made her sound so pathetic. He might as well call her a wimp, like Joss had. 'Why can't you just leave me alone, you great busybody?'

'Easy. I want to know what you were doing trampling round our garden, when now you're so keen to get away.'

Flora gave up. She was too tired to carry on the fight. OK, let Tan call her a wimp; she was, wasn't she? They had reached the gate and she pushed it open and held it for Tan.

'Come on then,' she said, sulkily. 'But won't your dad miss you?'

'If he does, he won't worry too much. He reckons I can look after myself.'

Flora blinked. It was so different from the way Libby cocooned Flora in concern and counted the minutes her daughter was off on her own.

'So what's wrong then?' demanded Tan when they had walked only a few paces.

Flora gave him a sidelong look. He had such an open look of real concern that she longed to tell him everything. But how could she? How could she explain that she was furious with Joss for suggesting that David and Libby were in love? For goodness' sake, they had known each other for less than a week! How could she have taken Joss so seriously? And what was so bad about it anyway? It was very insulting to David to be so mad. Flora couldn't explain even to herself why she found the idea so unnerving.

But Tan wasn't going to give up. She knew that much even if she had only known him for a few days. And she was desperate to tell someone how much she was hurting about her ruined plans.

Slowly, and with much pause for thought while she weeded out the bits she didn't want him to hear, Flora explained about the row with Joss and her plans to give up school.

'So you see, now there's no one to cover for me,' she said dismally. 'Because I'll never be able to make it up with Joss. So I shall just have to carry on going to school. And my eczema's been getting better just with the thought of not going!'

'Dad wouldn't have written that letter pretending your boat had moved on,' said Tan, thoughtfully. 'He'd have said it was lying. But there must be another way. We must be able to think of something.'

'Really?' said Flora, excitedly. 'You mean, you wouldn't mind helping me?' Her heart began to pound so hard at the thought of another way out that she felt quite sick.

"Course not,' said Tan. 'You think I want you to carry on being so miserable? Of course I'll help. But it'll have to be a secret. Dad mustn't find out; he'd insist on telling your mum.'

Flora's face fell. 'So what *can* I do? I've got to be educated. You said that was the law.'

'Easy. I just tell you to do the work I've done the day before.'

Flora blushed. 'Tan, I'm not as brainy as you. I can't even read and write properly.'

'OK, that's no problem. You can do things I would have done a while back.' Tan was striding out purposefully now, his lips pursed in a soundless whistle. Flora sighed. She was turning into one of his projects. She just hoped he didn't get bored with her, like some of the things he had been sorting out in his den the day she'd first met him.

'But how are we going to manage about the letter and everything?' Flora worried.

'I'm thinking about it. I'll tell you if I come up with anything in the morning.'

'In the morning?'

'At church. You'll be there, won't you?'

'Well, usually I stay with Joss… Oh…' Flora stopped, dismayed. Tan had got there before her. 'Well, yes, I suppose I will,' she mumbled.

'We could try praying about it,' said Tan, cheerily. 'That's what Dad would do.'

'What, d'you believe in God then?'

'I'm not sure yet,' said Tan. 'But there's no harm in trying, is there?'

7

Libby was very tight-lipped when Flora got back to the *Thorpe Cloud* and inclined to blame her daughter for the whole affair. That was until Flora, feeling very mean but not knowing how else to defend herself, told her some of what Joss had said.

'A scabby little drip!' Libby raged. 'How dare she? How low can you go, sneering at someone for something which isn't their fault?' Flora wondered if she meant the eczema or being a drip, but decided she'd rather not know.

'I've a good mind to go round and smack her myself. I'm sure she deserves it,' Libby ranted on. 'Dear me, it's not surprising Zilla's had so much trouble with that son of hers, if that's the way she lets her children carry on.'

'She was very upset,' said Flora, guiltily. 'She's never said anything like that before.'

'I should hope not,' retorted Libby. 'And I hope you've got the sense not to be friends with anyone else who calls you names. You mustn't stand for it, d'you hear me, Flora? I don't want you mixing with people with such awful prejudices.'

Well, that wipes out most of the kids at school, thought Flora, glumly. There were a few who made a big show of not keeping their distance when her eczema was at its worst, but most of them ignored her or even crossed the corridor when they saw her coming. And she'd heard all the names, even though they whispered sideways behind their fingers.

'I won't be able to go round there tomorrow,' Flora pointed out.

'Round where?' Libby looked blank.

'To Joss'. While you're at church.'

'Oh,' said Libby, the full implications of the row suddenly hitting her. Unless Joss and Flora made it up, there would be no quiet evenings with Flora aboard the *Argo*. And no free babysitting—not that that would have mattered a couple of weeks ago. 'Well, I suppose I don't have to go to church.' She twisted her fingers discontentedly.

'I could just go and say I'm sorry and try and make it all up,' volunteered Flora, scratching a wrist anxiously.

'No. Leave it for now. Give Joss a chance to calm down. Don't scratch, Flora.'

They sat and looked at each other, neither wanting to give way, Flora desperately trying to blank out of her mind the itching which seemed to be creeping over her entire body.

'I could try church,' said Flora, at last. 'Tan says it's not so bad. But I don't want to go to that Sunday School, all right?'

'You're a good kid, Flora,' said Libby, letting out a big sigh of relief. She gave Flora a quick hug. 'I'm sure you'll really like it when you get there.'

'Not the Sunday School,' said Flora firmly, wondering why it was quite so important for Libby not to miss church.

Libby smiled and ruffled her hair. 'I'm not deaf, you know. Though I can't think why you're so dead set against it.'

Flora sighed. She was so good at hiding her true feelings from Libby that sometimes she thought she knew nothing about her.

Tan was bouncing around in the churchyard when Libby and Flora arrived for the service the next morning.

'You decided to come then,' he said excitedly, as Flora walked sedately over to where he was hanging off a tombstone.

'I didn't have much choice,' she replied. 'Won't the vicar mind you doing that?'

'Don't see why,' said Tan, who was now balancing his way round a stone ledge surrounding a grave. 'If we're all going on to heaven or hell, there's nothing under this grass but bones.'

'But what about the people who come and put flowers here? Won't they be offended?'

'Oh pooh, Flora! Sometimes you're a real bore!'

Flora's lip trembled and she turned away. Yesterday a wimp and a drip, today a bore. Maybe she should just go and jump in the canal and stop irritating all the far more exciting people she had the misfortune to live with.

But Tan was too kind to leave her miserable for long.

'Sorry, Flora. I didn't mean it. I was just cross because you're right. Look, slap my face too if it'd make you feel better.'

Flora giggled. 'That's not funny,' she said, trying to be stern. 'And, anyway, you weren't as rude as Joss was. But you'd better watch out! Libby went mad when she heard what Joss called me. She says I'm not to mix with people who call me names.'

'Ooh! I'm shaking,' said Tan, with a grin. Then his

face suddenly seemed to broaden out, as if he had seen something new and wonderful. 'Flora, wait a minute!' he gasped. He grabbed her by the shoulder so hard that it hurt. 'Flora, that's it! That's your way out of school!'

'Stop shouting, Tan. Someone'll hear you. What d'you mean? What's my way out?'

'Oh crikey, the service will start in a minute. I'll have to tell you afterwards.'

'Tan, no! I can't wait! I'll *die* if you don't tell me now!'

Tan looked at her strained, white face and decided not to take the risk. Very quickly, he outlined his plan.

'I write a letter, OK, pretending it's from your mum. I say that for reasons I do not wish to discuss, I feel that you will be happier at a smaller school—or some sort of rubbish like that. I'll say that as there are only a few weeks left of the school year, I am keeping you at home from now on and I'd be glad if your books could be sent to me, so that you can continue with your lessons. How's that?'

'But that's lying too,' complained Flora. 'I don't get it. And won't the truant man come round and check up on me?'

'It's a bit of a lie,' admitted Tan, 'but not a really bad one. I mean, your mum actually said you're not to mix with people that call you names—and from what you say, they're nearly all like that at your school. Right?'

'Most of them,' agreed Flora.

'Well then? So really we're just doing what your mum wants—just without her having to be bothered with it all.'

'But what about the truant man?'

'Look, we'll have to go into church now. I'll tell you the rest later. Just don't worry about it, Flora. Trust me, OK?'

'Hmmph!' said Flora, unimpressed.

Flora worried about it so much that, even though it was her first time in church, she barely noticed what was going on.

She didn't just worry about what Tan had said either. She worried about everything there was to worry about—her eczema, her migraines, Joss, David and Libby, the fact that she still couldn't read well enough to sing from the church song-book—but most of all she worried about being a drip and a wimp and a bore. She was certainly a bore. It *was* boring to be scabby and ill half the time, but that wasn't all there was to it. She wasn't at all adventurous—perhaps she should blame Libby for that, always worried that she would drown in the canal or that a mad axe-man would get her—but whose fault was it that she wasn't bright and cheerful and colourful like Joss and Tan? OK, so she was quiet—but quiet didn't have to mean drip, did it? Quiet didn't mean she had to let other people walk all over her and organize her life, like Joss tended to and Tan obviously wanted to do. But she needed help and Tan had a plan, so if she just carried on going to school then she'd only be a different sort of wimp.

At that moment, a sudden sticky wetness under her fingernail brought her to her senses. She looked at her wrists in horror. Sure enough, locked in her thoughts, she had done her worst—scratched and scratched till she had drawn blood—and in a summer frock with no long sleeves to pull down and cover the damage. Libby would go bananas. Furtively, Flora rummaged in her pocket and—phew!—found a clean handkerchief. She wrapped it tightly round the bleeding wrist and twisted the ends round and round so that the pressure from the makeshift bandage almost deadened the itching. She threw her head up and did her utmost to concentrate on the service.

The vicar was reading from the Bible. It was a story about Jesus, one Flora had never heard before, not that she'd heard very many. She listened. It was pleasant to be read to by someone other than Libby, and Flora liked the story. It was about a little girl who was so very ill that whilst her father was hurrying to bring Jesus to her, she died. Well, that's what everyone thought had happened, anyway. Flora wondered if she had just slipped into a coma. When Jesus arrived, he brushed all the mourners aside. 'Get up, my child,' he said. And she did.

Flora sighed. She wished the story had gone on longer. She felt all warm and comfortable, like she did the first time Libby had read *A Little Princess* and she had heard how Sara Crewe had found her father's friend in the house next door. If someone was going to read stories at church, she would come every week. She sat very still whilst all the other children scrambled out of their pews to go to the Sunday School. She wanted the lovely, cosy feeling to last as long as possible.

Libby glanced at her and decided not to say anything. Why force her to go to Sunday School if she didn't want to? She seemed happy enough. And now there was this row with Joss. What a funny little kid she was, though. She wondered if God had listened to all the prayers she had said for her in the last few weeks.

'Oh well,' thought Libby, 'Time to try again.'

'Well, was it as bad as you thought it would be?' demanded Tan, bounding up to Flora at the end of the service.

'N-o-o...' said Flora. 'I quite liked it actually. And I tried praying. I thought I might as well give it a go.'

'So? Did anything happen?'

'I'm not sure yet,' said Flora, thoughtfully. 'But I'm not as worried as I was.'

'Well, I told you not to worry.'

'I know. But I didn't take any notice.'

'Oh,' said Tan, looking bemused. He decided to change the subject. 'So what about my plan? What do you think?'

Flora shook her head. 'I'm not sure,' she said. 'What about the truant man?'

'Oh, that's easy. By the time he's caught up with you—he's called the Educational Welfare Officer, by the way—it'll be the summer holidays. And I'll say in the letter that you're going to a private establishment—which is true in a way.'

'What's "establishment" mean?'

'Well, just a sort of building, I think. It could be a school—or it *could* be just a house. They'll think it's a school, of course, and if you go to a private school then the EWO doesn't have to bother with you any more—he only has to worry about the kids that go to state schools. You'll just get forgotten, I'm sure.'

'I don't think so.' Flora shook her head again. 'They're bound to send a letter home.'

'So? The postman doesn't come to your boat, does he? Who collects the letters from the post office?'

'I do. On the way home from school. Mum occasionally goes and gets them early if she's expecting something.'

'Oh. How often does that happen?'

'I told you. Only occasionally.'

Tan sighed and rubbed his forehead with his hand. 'Oh well, I suppose we'll just have to chance it. It should be easy, though. We'll just open any letters which come from your school and deal with them.'

'I don't see how,' objected Flora. 'How would we know which they were?'

'Oh, they're bound to have something written on the envelope like Oxfordshire Education Authority or something. You do fuss, Flora.'

'No, I don't. I just want to make sure this is going to work.' She glared at him. *There!* Flora thought. *You can't call that wimpish or boring. It's just common sense.*

Tan pulled a face. 'Well, I'm sure we'll be able to tell. You could try praying again, seeing as you seemed to like it so much.'

'I didn't say that!'

'No, but you looked as pleased as Punch when you came out of church.'

'Did I?'

'Yes. Don't hit me. It's not an insult.'

Flora relaxed. She hadn't meant to sound cross; she was just surprised. She *had* felt better when she came out of church—stronger, somehow. Maybe it had the same effect on Libby; maybe that was why she kept going.

'Anyway,' continued Tan, 'all we have to do now is work out how you're going to cover up on the school bus. Then you can just come along to my den every day and get on with whatever you want to do.'

'Whatever I want to do?'

'Yes, why not? That's the way I get on, most of the time, though Dad does make sure I keep doing a bit of the basic stuff—you know, writing, spelling, maths. The rest of the time I just work on what I'm interested in.'

'Wow!' said Flora. She could hardly wait to start. Her brain suddenly felt so crowded with things she'd like to have a go at, she could almost hear it fizzing. 'If I can't think of anything else, I'll just get the bus every morning and then walk straight back,' she said fiercely. 'I know loads of ways through the fields so no one will spot me.'

'Are you sure?' said Tan. 'It's a long way.'

'It's nothing,' said Flora, her head held very high. 'I've done it loads of times.'

'But what about the bus home?'

'Oh, Joss won't notice if I'm not there,' said Flora, drunk with the excitement of her plan. 'She sits upstairs with her friends on the way back. She doesn't like to be seen with me too much.'

'I don't know...'

'Now who's making a fuss?' said Flora, impatiently. 'Half the time I'm not even there! She's used to me bunking off, OK?'

'Well, all right. If you're sure.'

'I am sure. So that's settled then, OK?' The look in her eyes dared Tan to disagree.

'Crikey!' said Tan. 'We'd better start work on the letter.'

8

In the end Flora insisted on writing the letter herself, or at least painstakingly typing out what she and Tan had agreed on his ancient typewriter.

'It'd better be me that does it,' she said, firmly. 'I mean, it's me that doesn't want to go to school.'

It took her two days to get it perfect and Tan had to go with her to the postbox, as she suddenly got last-minute nerves. Her hand shook so much that he thought she'd never get the letter in the slot. In the end he gave her arm a helpful shove in the right direction.

'There! Done!' he said cheerfully. 'I'll buy you some chocolate to celebrate.'

Shakily, Flora followed him. She was so light-headed with a mixture of excitement and dread that she could barely walk in a straight line.

They sat on the bridge by the shop to eat their chocolate. Flora was still so worked up she hardly noticed it as she bolted it down. Tan, however, chomped slowly, busily working things out.

'OK, so if the letter takes two days to get there, that'll be Thursday, which means there'll only be a day before the weekend for them to ask you any awkward questions and then that'll be it! I'll see you in the den on Monday! I told you it'd be easy!'

Flora, however, wasn't so sure. What on earth would

she say on Friday? What if they asked her which 'private establishment' she was going to? What if they wanted to know Libby's reasons? Supposing Flora had to go to see the headteacher for one of her little heart-to-heart chats? (Please, God, if you're there, anything but that.)

She was very quiet by the time she got back to the *Thorpe Cloud* and it was a struggle to eat her tea.

'Are you feeling all right?' asked Libby suspiciously, inspecting her daughter's face for the tell-tale whiteness. 'Are you still upset about Joss? Have you talked to her yet?'

'I'm fine,' Flora lied. Like most migraine sufferers she refused to believe it was going to happen again until she was on the point of collapse.

Libby watched her play with her food and noted her unnatural quietness.

'Flora,' she said, gently. 'David says that if it's a migraine, you should go and lie down in the dark and take your medicine as soon as you think it's starting.'

'I'm *all right*!' Flora insisted with one last, superhuman effort, before the pain zinged in from a corner of the ceiling somewhere above her left eye and she went stumbling towards the loo, tears pouring down her face.

'Oh, Flora,' Libby sighed when she had mopped her up and tucked her into bed with a cold flannel across her forehead. 'Whatever are we going to do with you?'

'Try... praying,' mumbled Flora, thickly, which sent Libby scurrying to the First Aid box for a thermometer to see if her daughter was delirious.

Flora woke the next morning, gagging on the smell of freshly-brewed coffee. She was dimly aware that it was David who held the bowl for her and wiped her face again.

'Sorry, love,' he said, softly. 'I shouldn't have made the coffee. I just dropped by and Libby asked me to stay while she nipped down to the post office. She'll be back soon.'

Flora didn't care. She relaxed under his gentle touch and let sleep well up and save her from the pain.

All morning she slept fitfully, but without needing the bowl again.

It was afternoon when she woke properly. Her head felt better and she lay very still, waiting to see what her tummy would do.

From the kitchen area, she could hear voices.

'But what if it isn't migraine?' Libby was saying. 'What if it's something worse? Could there be something wrong with her brain? I mean, she's never done well at school and for the life of me I can't see why—I mean, she was such a bright toddler. And she doesn't seem stupid to me now. But she is rather odd sometimes, especially just recently. All this trouble with Joss, for example. She hasn't even tried to make it up, as far as I know. And last night she told me to try praying! I mean, she's never, ever mentioned God or praying in her whole life as far as I know.'

'Well, you did take her to church on Sunday.' It was David. Again.

'I know, but I didn't expect it to have any *effect*.'

David burst out laughing and then immediately tried to quieten down. 'Why on earth not? It's had an effect on you, hasn't it?'

'Well, yes—sort of—but she's just a little girl.'

'Oh, I see. God's only for grown-ups, right?'

'I didn't mean that! Oh, you're as bad as Tan sometimes, always putting me on the spot.' Flora heard something that sounded distinctly like Libby slamming down a coffee mug.

'OK, OK, back to the migraine,' said David, soothingly. 'Well, look. You can always ask to have her checked over by a neurologist—but I honestly believe it's migraine. She was sick when I brewed fresh coffee this morning and Tan said she had some chocolate last night. They can both trigger it off. And there's the row with Joss. Stress just makes it all worse.'

'But she's *always* getting migraines! Surely she can't always be stressed out?'

'It could be school that's doing it,' said David, in a casual voice.

'Now don't start,' said Libby, her voice tightening. 'You know what I think of that and I don't care what you say about how brilliantly it's working with Tan; I am not having Flora educated at home. She's different enough from other children as it is…'

Flora decided she didn't want to hear any more. It made her heart pound and her stomach churn. There was no way Tan could pretend their letter wasn't the biggest lie she had ever told. Libby might not want her mixing with kids who called her names but she did want her to go to school.

'Mum!' she called, weakly, 'Mum!' Straightaway Libby appeared, with David close behind her.

Under David's instruction, Flora had to take her medicine now that her stomach was behaving itself, drink some water and then lie down again, while Libby bathed her face with a clean-smelling lotion called witch hazel. It was all very soothing. Libby was much calmer and gentler with David around. Perhaps it wouldn't be so very bad if they did fall in love? But Flora quickly chased that thought from her brain. It was too big to think about now.

It was the next day before Flora was fit to get up, despite all David's advice. It had been a very bad attack. David had given Libby a pile of old magazines from Migraine Action and Libby had been reading them avidly in her free moments. Reassured that Flora wasn't about to die from a mysterious brain disease, she was keen to try out everything she'd read.

'We'll start with your diet,' she told Flora enthusiastically, as Flora flopped her head down on the table, having pushed her plate aside. 'We'll try cutting out one thing at a time. I think the first had better be chocolate, seeing as you don't drink coffee. Then we could try cheese. How d'you feel about that?'

Flora groaned. 'I don't care,' she said and at that moment, she didn't. She felt too limp and exhausted to be bothered. What she wouldn't give for a soak in David's huge bath! A shower was too much like hard work; she would just crawl off back to bed again.

Flora woke the next morning to bright summer sunshine which didn't hurt, so she knew she was nearly better. For the first time since the pain had begun, she wondered if Libby would send her to school today or whether… No, it would be too good to be true, on this day of all days, the very day when any awkward questions might be asked, if Libby decided to send her to David's.

Her stomach gave a little flutter and she clutched at it nervously. No, she wasn't going to be sick; it was just excitement. Today was her last school day—and she might even be going to miss it!

An hour later, walking along the tow-path with Tan, she could barely stop herself from leaping in the air for joy. NO MORE SCHOOL! She wasn't to go today; Libby had insisted that she take things easy, so here she was on her way to Buxton House. All Flora's guilty doubts were quashed. She was free! Whole years of feeling stupid and keeping quiet for fear of looking an idiot seemed to unroll themselves and slither into the cool, dark depths of the canal to be lost forever. She could be the real Flora again.

'Hey, watch out, Flora!' called Tan as she skipped and bounced along in front of him. 'You're so high, you'll fall in the canal if you're not careful!'

'Then I'll swim to the bank!' she called gaily and continued her giddy progress.

'My goodness, you do look better!' exclaimed David when he saw Flora. 'But I think Libby's right to keep you off school just one more day. Then you'll have the weekend, so by Monday you'll be as right as rain.'

Flora and Tan exchanged glances. Flora could hardly suppress a gleeful giggle, so it was a good job David had turned away to root around in the fridge. Triumphantly he produced a tiny, plastic box full of small, speckled eggs and placed them on the table amidst an array of other strange foodstuffs.

'Quails' eggs,' he said. 'Only from Sainsbury's, I'm afraid, but the genuine article just the same. We were hoping you'd be well enough to join us today—we're going to cook a Tudor banquet. D'you think we'll be able to drag Libby away from her typewriter tonight?'

Flora grinned delightedly. 'Don't give her a choice,' she said.

* * *

In an office at Flora's school, Stanley Hobbs, Educational Welfare Officer, was carrying out his weekly inspection of the school's registers. So Flora Adams was absent for a third day. That was peculiar. He'd been keeping an eye on Flora's absences for some time now. They were frequent, but usually only a day at a time—but there had been a two-day gap only last week, he was sure. He checked through the pile of notes at the back of the register. Yes, he was right—a typewritten letter excusing a two-day absence because of migraine. It was usually migraine that kept her away, wasn't it? Yes, migraine or trips to consultants about her eczema—the odd dentist's appointment, of course, and an assortment of colds and twenty-four hour bugs. Poor little scrap! He'd seen her a couple of times and she never looked well but...? Could so many absences be genuine? Why were some typed and some written by hand? No, he was being silly. He had enough problems with other more difficult children, without agonizing over little Flora Adams. And yet...

'Here's one less for you to worry about,' said a voice over his shoulder. It was Flora's class teacher and she was brandishing a letter. 'Here. Read this. Flora Adams is leaving and it sounds like she's going to some private school, though where the money's coming from I wouldn't know. She's on free school meals. Her mother's a dark horse, though. It wouldn't surprise me if she had pots of money stashed away. Living on a narrow boat could be an artistic pose. She's a writer, you know.'

'Really?' said Stanley Hobbs, scanning the letter he'd been given. It was well written—it could easily have been composed by someone who was a writer—but the signature? He compared it with a couple of the notes from the register. Was it the same? He wished he had a magnifying glass.

'Oh well,' he said, handing the letter back. 'I suppose you're right. One less to worry about. You can't persuade a few more to leave, can you?'

But he still wasn't sure. Somehow, something didn't seem quite right. Something he couldn't quite put his finger on. Yet.

9

Flora curled up happily in the big armchair in Tan's den and opened her book. It had only taken a few days for her to realize that, if she chose carefully from Tan's huge pile of books and took her time, here were books that she could read.

'I don't understand,' she told Tan. 'I couldn't have read this to my teacher at school. Or to Mum. Well, I haven't tried to read to Mum for ages, actually—it always ended in a row.'

'Maybe that's it,' said Tan, with a shrug. 'Maybe they make you panic so your brain won't work properly. Anyway, you can do it now, so what's the problem?'

'I wouldn't say I can *do* it, exactly,' Flora corrected him. 'But I'm getting much better. And it's so lovely and peaceful here. I can really concentrate.'

'So it's working!' said Tan, jubilantly. 'Even if someone does find out, they can't make you go back to school when you're doing so well here! And that's only after a few days!'

'I'm not so sure,' said Flora, but quickly decided not to think about it.

Today she was reading a book she had heard all the other kids talking about and had longed to be able to read herself—*The Angel of Nitshill Road*. She couldn't quite believe she was actually reading it. It was as if the angel had come out of the book and sorted out all her problems too.

A little shiver ran down her spine. What if… what if… what if it wasn't just the peace and quiet of the den that was helping her? What if—she thought about how she had prayed in church—what if it had WORKED?

She quickly turned back to her book. She preferred not to dwell on it. It was all getting a bit too fantastic. Anyway, Tan was probably right. No teacher making her panic and lots of time to concentrate. That was why her reading was coming on so quickly.

And everything else was going so well, too. Each morning she dawdled along behind all the others as they hurried off the school bus and in through the gate. No one seemed to think it was odd; they all knew about the row with Joss. Flora lurked around the old bicycle shed that hardly anyone used and then, as soon as everyone was out of sight, she started her journey back. She was lucky that the school didn't have a uniform and was right on the edge of a village, but it was still rather an awkward walk, especially at the end, where she couldn't use the tow-path past the *Thorpe Cloud*, or the road through the village. Fortunately she had found a path which led off the main road and joined the tow-path at Buxton Tunnel, but it was very little used. For the first few days, Flora arrived at the den covered in nettle rash. Now, however, she had trampled down the undergrowth and it was a helpful short cut.

There had been one letter from the school. Flora had made Tan collect the post with her each day, as she wasn't sure her reading was up to recognizing a school envelope, but when it did arrive it was perfectly obvious. It was huge because it contained Flora's exercise books and had been franked with the school's name and logo right across the top. The letter was very long and there were lots of big words which Flora didn't understand, but the only bit which worried them was where it asked for the name and address of Flora's new school so that her records could be sent on.

'Crikey!' said Tan. 'I didn't think of that. Now what are we going to do?'

Flora's heart sank. If Tan didn't know what to do, what chance was there of her coming up with something? But she wasn't going to give up that easily. Not any more. She racked her brains.

'Easy!' she cried suddenly, surprising herself. 'We write and tell them we haven't decided which school to send me to yet and we'll let them know when we have. If we leave it long enough, they might even forget about me.'

'More lies,' said Tan, dubiously. 'I thought you…'

'Don't start that,' said Flora, firmly. 'You were the one that said it was all OK because really my mum doesn't want me at school.'

'I know but…'

'Oh, stop arguing and let's get the letter written,' snapped Flora.

So Tan had worked out what they should say and Flora had painstakingly typed it and so far they had heard nothing further. Meanwhile Flora's eczema was calming down and she hadn't had a migraine since she had 'left' school. She was so happy that she ate better, slept better and even looked better.

'Flora's changed a lot in the last few weeks,' she heard David saying to Libby one day. 'She's looking much healthier.'

'Really?' said Libby, glancing across at her. 'I can't say I've noticed, but then I'm with her so much. It's like when they're babies and everyone keeps telling you how much they've grown.'

Flora spent a long time looking in the mirror that night. Her face seemed a bit plumper and her hair had more bounce. Was it so obvious? Libby clearly hadn't really noticed, but supposing Flora kept on improving? Supposing Libby started asking awkward questions?

'Tan,' Flora said worriedly the next day. 'Do I look different now I've stopped going to school?'

Tan studied her critically for a moment. 'Yes,' he said definitely. 'Yes, you do.'

'So you'd notice? I mean, so Libby would notice and start wondering why?'

'I'm not sure. I don't think so,' said Tan, continuing to weigh her up. 'I mean it's not something dead obvious—she might just think you were growing up.'

'Why? What is it that's different? All I can see is that my face looks fatter. I'm worried, Tan. I mean, I'm glad my skin's so much better and everything, but I don't want Libby getting suspicious.'

'Well, don't worry about it. You'll only get a migraine. It's nothing much really. You just look—well…'

'What, Tan, what?'

'Prettier. That's all. Just a bit prettier.'

'Ooh.' Flora covered her burning cheeks with her hands. A bit prettier. Never had such a tiny compliment meant so much.

So here she was in the middle of her fifth week in the den, enjoying her book, happier, healthier and prettier. Sometimes her stomach churned as she hurried towards Buxton House in the morning, from the sheer excitement of spending another day in the den, choosing what she wanted to do. So far, whatever she had needed Tan had been able to provide, be it books, paper, glue, scissors, paint, a cassette radio—he even brought her sandwiches at lunchtime.

'Doesn't your dad notice?' asked Flora, worriedly.

'He just thinks I'm extra hungry,' said Tan. 'I'm a growing lad, you know.'

Whenever he could, he came to join her, playing board games or getting on with his own things. At four o'clock, of course, all the hiding could stop and they were free to do as they liked.

Sometimes Flora thought guiltily about Joss. She had never gone round to try to make it up. She couldn't. And Joss had said nothing to her either. But she didn't seem very happy. She had always laughed and chatted to the other kids on the school bus and had made a big show of doing so for a week or more after the row. But now she seemed quiet and withdrawn—and on the nights when the band jammed, Flora couldn't hear much flute. Flora put it down to the boat yard closing. That's what she hoped anyway.

Footsteps crunched on the gravel. Lost in her book, Flora jumped. But it was all right. It was only Tan. He burst through the door, streaming warm summer rain from his cagoule and rapidly creating a puddle on the small patch of floor.

'Tan! You're soaked!' exclaimed Flora.

'Yes, and I'm fed up,' he said grumpily, hauling off his cagoule and flinging it over the desk. 'Dad just told me to go away and not come back until I was in a pleasanter frame of mind. So I'm here. Wet. Where can I sit?'

Flora looked about the cramped space. Seeing as he had just dripped all over the only free bit of floor and his cagoule covered the desk and seat, it wasn't an easy question to answer.

'Here?' she suggested finally, standing up.

'Don't be stupid. You're sitting there.'

This wasn't like Tan at all. Flora sat down again, perplexed.

'What's the matter, Tan?' she said, nervously. 'Didn't you enjoy the trip to the castle? Did the rain ruin it?'

'No, it was fine,' said Tan, crossly. 'In fact, it was brilliant. I found out loads of stuff.'

He threw his cagoule on the floor and sat on the damp desk. 'But that was just the trouble. All the time, I kept thinking, 'Gosh, Flora would really like this. Wow! I must remember to tell Flora about that,' until in the end, I felt so bad about you being stuck in this shed whilst I was out with my friends on a trip to a castle, that I just wanted to come home.'

'Oh no!' said Flora, her heart sinking. He mustn't ruin his trips out worrying about her; what if it put him off the whole scheme?

'I don't mind, Tan,' she said, quickly. 'Honestly I don't. I love it here. I knew you'd be going off on trips some of the time—it's fine. Really it is. I thought you knew that.'

'I know. I know what you said. But I just don't see how it can be true. How can you be happy, stuck in here all day?' Tan pushed back his damp fringe fretfully.

'I *am* happy. You can see I'm happy. Look! Look at my skin. I haven't scratched for days. Honestly Tan, I'd far rather be here than stuck in school. Other kids might get lonely here but I love it.'

76

Tan wiped his nose on the back of his hand. 'You mean that? You're not just saying it to shut me up?'

'I mean it. I promise.'

But Tan still wasn't satisfied. He got up and paced about on the damp square of floor. 'But it's not going to work,' he said, despairingly. 'You've got to go out and see things. You've got to meet other people. I mean, there'll be days when I have friends over and you won't be able to join in, you'll be stuck in this shed.'

Flora shrugged. 'I'll be fine. I don't mind that, honestly. And you never know—maybe one day...' She stopped, her face suddenly flushing. No, she wasn't going to even think that thought, let alone say it.

'Maybe one day what?' said Tan, looking at her oddly.

'Nothing,' said Flora, firmly. 'I'm going to be just fine. And I'm going to make this home-education thing work out for me too, so stop fussing, OK?'

Tan shrugged. 'OK, your majesty,' he said wryly. 'Anything you say. And you think *I'm* bossy!'

10

Flora fidgeted in her bunk. She couldn't get to sleep. It was a warm, sultry August night and for the first time since 'leaving' school, her eczema was playing up. Libby had opened the door of the cabin in an attempt to create a draught and, resonant in the heavy night air, Flora could hear the sounds of Joss' family and friends jamming. She could hear laughter and the clink of glasses. She could hear Reuben's accordion and Zilla's violin and frequent bursts of singing. But no flute.

Flora put her hands behind her head and worried. What was wrong with Joss? Zilla had told Libby that it wasn't absolutely definite that the boat yard would close—all sorts of unexpected people were protesting about it—so why was Joss so glum? Could she be worried about going to secondary school, only a few weeks away now? Flora found that hard to believe; Joss did well in her lessons and had always been confident. Surely it couldn't be because of Flora? But what else could it be?

Tonight was just the sort of night when Flora would have loved to slip over to the *Argo* and listen and watch till she fell asleep. But all that had ceased. Reuben had stopped her once on the tow-path.

'We don't see much of you now, Flora,' he'd said. 'We miss you, you know. And not just Zilla and me.'

Flora hadn't known what to say and had stood there smiling foolishly.

'Oh well,' said Reuben. 'Just remember we're here if you ever want to come and talk about it, OK?'

Flora nodded dumbly and Reuben cycled off, his massive frame looking dangerously top-heavy on his bicycle.

Flora didn't like thinking about it. It hurt somewhere deep in her chest when she thought of Reuben's big, kindly face smiling down at her in that puzzled way. If only she could turn the clock back and unsay all those stupid things she had said to Joss and didn't have to know that Joss thought she was a scabby little drip. Because that was the trouble. Even if she went and grovelled to Joss, she could never forgive her for saying that.

Flora ground her teeth in the dark. If only Joss was still her friend, life would be perfect. Four more weeks of the summer holidays stretched ahead and, much as she loved her time in the den, it was glorious not to have to hide away or worry about being caught.

Thinking about the den sent a little thrill of pleasure running up her spine. She couldn't believe how much better she felt and how much faster she could read. On one never-to-be-forgotten July morning, she had suddenly realized that she had got through a whole chapter without noticing that she was reading. She hadn't paused to struggle with a single word.

'I can read,' she announced excitedly to Tan when he appeared at lunch-time.

'So what's new? I know you can,' he said, bored.

'No, I mean I can *really* read,' she insisted. 'Listen.'

And she read a whole chapter to him without hesitating or stumbling once.

'Brilliant!' he said when she'd finished, almost as excited as she was. 'No one could send you back now.'

And indeed, no one had tried. The remaining days of the summer term had passed without anything further from the school, apart from a note to say that their last letter had arrived and had been put on file.

So now it was wonderful—except for Joss—and except for David and... Flora rolled over and shut her eyes determinedly. She was *not* going to think about it.

It seemed that Flora had no sooner closed her eyes than she was awake again, her space lit up by a vivid streak of lightning. The boat seemed to rock when the thunder crash came hard after it. Flora dived under her cover. She hated being on a narrow boat in a storm. It all sounded so close.

'You all right, Flora?' It was Libby.

Flora peered over the top of the duvet and shook her head.

'I'll make a drink,' said Libby and Flora hid and shivered until her mum returned with two mugs of Horlicks and a packet of digestive biscuits. They huddled together on the bunk and drank and munched companionably until the storm began to move away.

'All right now?' said Libby, feeling Flora's head growing heavier against her shoulder.

'Mmm,' said Flora, sleepily. 'I do love you, Mum. Best in all the world.'

Libby slipped off the bunk and snuggled the duvet round Flora again.

'I love you too, poppet,' she said. 'And don't you forget it.'

Flora awoke bad-tempered. She had slept so heavily

after the storm that her head ached and she had thoughtlessly scratched her wrists whilst worrying about Joss, so now they were red and inflamed. Then she remembered that it was Sunday.

She had been going to church for some weeks now—there wasn't really any choice—and, although it had never seemed quite as special as the first time, she was enjoying it. She loved the music and found there was always something entertaining to watch before the children went out to Sunday School. After that, although sometimes she got a bit bored, she liked experimenting with the odd prayer and puzzling over the Bible that sat on the ledge in front of her.

But this morning she didn't want to go. She felt heavy and cross and tired and she didn't want anyone to see her wrists. She had got used to having clear skin and didn't want to go back. *A scabby little drip*. The words haunted her.

And there was another reason.

'Do we have to go to church this morning?' she demanded, watching Libby putting on her make-up.

'Why not?' said Libby, surprised. 'I thought you liked it. It seemed to make a big impression on you that first time.'

'Well, I don't want to go this morning. Can't we stay at home and make fudge or something? We haven't done anything like that for weeks. And we still haven't finished *A Little Princess*.'

Libby frowned. 'Can't we do that some other time, Flora? It's not as if we haven't read it before.'

'When?' demanded Flora. 'This afternoon?'

Libby hesitated. 'Well, no, not this afternoon. David suggested we might go to the open-air pool and then

81

have a barbecue. I thought you'd like that.'

'You never asked me.'

'No, I know—but you weren't there to ask. And you've always liked swimming.'

'With you,' said Flora, pointedly.

'Well, you'll be with me.'

'Not really. You'll be with David. Chatting to him all the time. You'll want me to go off and play with Tan.'

'Not all the time. That's not fair. And anyway, you like Tan. I thought he was your best friend. And you like David. Don't you?'

'Ye-e-s.' Flora couldn't pretend that she didn't.

'So what's the problem?'

'Oh, I don't know.' To her horror, Flora found she was having to blink back tears. What was wrong with her? Libby was quite right. She did like Tan and she did like David—and she didn't want to be mean and stop Libby from being in love with David, if that's what she really wanted—but it used to be just her and Libby and that had been special in a funny sort of way and...

'Oh, I just don't want to go to church today, that's all,' she burst out. 'Can't we just miss it for once?'

Libby looked at her carefully. 'You're not getting a migraine, are you? You look really tired.'

Flora shook her head vigorously.

'OK, we'll give it a miss this week and we'll do what you want—but I don't want to make a habit of it, OK?'

'OK,' said Flora. 'Thanks.'

Curled up with Libby later, listening to the adventures of the Little Princess, Flora tried to ignore the warning signs for as long as possible. This one precious morning she had snatched to be alone with Libby—it

82

couldn't end with her huddled in bed, blinded by pain.

But it could.

'Oh, Flora,' said Libby, despairingly. 'When will you learn to take your medicine earlier? Why didn't you say, you silly girl?'

'Didn't want it to happen,' mumbled Flora. 'Sorry.'

'But David says it might *not* happen, if you take your medicine soon enough.'

But David says... Flora groaned. Perhaps she deserved to be holed up like this on a lovely, sunny afternoon when she could be at the outdoor pool. She hated herself for being so mean and jealous. Perhaps she should try praying.

'Dear God...' she began in her head. But that was as far as she got. The medicine Libby had forced down her had begun to take effect and the pain ebbed just enough for her to fall into a fretful, fitful sleep.

11

'Flora! Wake up! Come and look at this!'

Flora groaned and opened one eye. Libby was standing over her, brandishing the local newspaper.

'Oh, I'm sorry, love,' she said, contritely. 'I forgot about your poor head—I was so excited! How are you feeling?'

Flora blinked and considered how she felt.

'I think I'm all right,' she said, blearily. 'What is it?'

'The boat yard has been saved—well, nearly.'

Flora's heart leaped. She sat up more suddenly than she should have done. Her head wasn't perfect yet.

'How?' she demanded. 'What's happened?' Her mind was racing. If the boat yard was safe, maybe Joss would be OK again. All the uncertainty must have been very unsettling. Maybe...

'There's a plan to keep it as a working boat yard, but to make it into a tourist attraction as well—you know, smarten it up and make it into a little waterways museum, that sort of thing. It's not settled yet. They need planning permission and what-have-you—but it looks pretty certain to go ahead—if you can believe what it says in this rag. It sounds brilliant. What a relief for Zilla and Reuben. Flora? Are you all right?'

Flora had sunk back down on her bunk. 'I'm fine,' she lied. 'It's just my head. Thanks for telling me. It's great news.'

But really there was a nasty, hard knot of misery inside her. *A scabby little drip*. She still couldn't forget it, or all the other things Joss had said. She just couldn't. The *Argo* would stay but the awfulness would go on for ever.

Flora rolled onto her tummy, buried her face in her pillow and cried.

She languished in bed all morning, but just before lunch Tan arrived. Could she cope with Tan today? Her mood was so black, she didn't feel like speaking to anyone. She lay where she was and listened to what he was saying to Libby.

'Is Flora well enough to come over for the afternoon? We've been to the pick-your-own and we've got *loads* of strawberries. We're going to make ice-cream and jam.'

'I'm coming,' called Flora and leaped out of bed. She'd never made jam or ice-cream. There was no storage space for jam on the *Thorpe Cloud* and it was a fight to get a packet of frozen peas into the ice-box of the tiny fridge. Her bad mood forgotten, she pulled on her clothes.

'Heard about the boat yard?' enquired Tan, as they strolled along the tow-path.

'Mmm,' said Flora, uninvitingly. She didn't want to talk about it.

Tan looked sideways at her, noted the stubborn look on her face and changed the subject. He was beginning to learn that Flora's obstinacy could be a match for his curiosity.

Buxton House was in view when Flora suddenly clutched Tan's arm.

'Look!' she hissed. 'At the end of the tunnel. It's Joss!'
'So?'

'But who's that with her?'

'I can't see anyone,' said Tan.

'I did. I'm sure I did.'

At that moment, Joss emerged from the gloom of the tunnel. She was alone.

'Funny,' said Flora. 'I was sure there was someone with her.'

'Probably just a shadow,' said Tan, dismissively. 'It's hard to see inside the tunnel from here. Anyway, what if there was?'

Flora didn't say anything. She was *certain* she had seen someone. Joss barely seemed to speak to anyone these days. It was distinctly odd, whatever Tan said.

Meanwhile, Joss was stomping towards them, her head down.

She glanced up as she approached, the way you always do when you sense there's someone coming. Flora could tell immediately that she wished she and Tan were a hundred miles away.

'Hi,' said Joss, tersely.

'Hi,' replied Flora and Tan.

'It's great news about the boat yard,' Tan added, rather too brightly.

'What's it to you?' said Joss, rudely, and walked on.

'Hey!' shouted Flora, and grabbed at Joss' arm so hard that she skidded in the dirt. 'There's no need to be horrible to Tan, even if you don't like me any more. He was only trying to be friendly.'

'Well, I don't need his friendship,' snapped Joss. 'Unlike you, of course. Don't think I don't know what you're up to, skiving off school every day. I've watched you hanging around till you think no one's looking and then skulking off back home. I suppose you go and hide at his house all day. It's a good job there's no one on our bus who's in your class or everyone'd know by now. Didn't you think that anyone'd notice? All the teachers think you've left but you still keep catching the bus every morning? Didn't you think that might seem a bit odd? And you forgot about the bus home again, didn't you? 'Course, half the time you're not on it anyway, 'cos you've bunked off—but every night? D'you think I'm blind or something? And what are you going to do in September when you need a new bus pass? Forge one?'

Flora stood rigid on the tow-path, her heart pounding.

'You won't…' All pride forgotten, she was going to beg Joss not to give her away.

'Tell?' sneered Joss. 'No, if I was going to tell, I'd have done it weeks ago. You ought to thank me for keeping quiet.'

'Ignore her, Flora,' Tan said, fiercely. 'She's just trying to wind you up. And for your information, Joss Robinson, she doesn't just hide at my house; she's carrying on her education. And even if you did go and split on her, I don't suppose it'd make any difference 'cos she's doing so well that no one would *want* her to go back to school! OK?'

'Oh yeah?' retorted Joss. 'Expect me to believe that? I've known Flora years longer than you have and I know what she's like. She can't even…'

'Stop!' Flora screamed. 'You don't know anything about me, Joss Robinson, not any more! I don't suppose you ever did, really. And if you don't clear off and leave me alone I'll… ' Flora paused, looking around desperately for inspiration.

'Push you in the canal!' Tan finished for her.

'Yes,' agreed Flora. 'I'll push you in the canal.'

Joss weighed them up. Tan was skinny and Flora was small but they would do it all right, she was sure of that.

'Two against one?' she sneered. 'What heroes!'

But she turned on her heel and walked away.

As soon as she was out of sight, Flora sat down hard in the middle of the tow-path and burst into tears.

'She used to be my *friend*!' she howled.

'Some friend!' muttered Tan, crouching down and putting an arm round her.

'But she never used to be like this! I know you don't believe me, but she used to be nice and kind and we did all sorts of lovely things together.'

Tan patted her helplessly. It was hard to imagine. The Joss he had met had always been sulky and unpleasant.

Flora wiped her nose on her sleeve.

'There's something funny going on,' she said, firmly. 'I'm sure of it. It can't just be the boat yard—especially not now it's going to be saved.'

'You did have a bit of a row with her, remember,' said Tan, tentatively.

'Yes, I know,' said Flora, irritably. 'But that's no reason for her to be so rotten to you, is it? No, there's more to it than that, I'm sure of it.'

12

The summer holidays slipped away. For the first time ever, Flora didn't count the final days of August with increasing dread. Instead, she felt a quiet sense of happy anticipation. The holidays had been lovely, apart from the fact that Libby and David had spent more and more time together and, of course, the trouble with Joss, but Flora was quite ready to settle into her routine of long, quiet hours in the den. Now that she could read fluently, she was devouring books. She had even reread *A Little Princess* from cover to cover on her own. After all, Libby never seemed to have time any more. Flora could hardly wait for the cool days of autumn, when she could curl up cosily with a book, without interruptions for trips to the open-air swimming pool and days out in the countryside. Not that she hadn't enjoyed herself. But she was ready for a change.

It was the first day of September. Flora woke early, chilly without the duvet she had thrown off the night before. She could hear the dull thuddety-thud of Libby, already at work at her typewriter, and the keen, morning light had lit up the whole cabin. It was impossible to go back to sleep. Flora studied her watch. She still struggled with telling the time. Almost seven o'clock. Libby wouldn't want to be disturbed. Perhaps she should just stay in bed and read?

But the late summer light called to her.

I know! she decided. *I'll give Tan and David an early call. David's always up early. Maybe he'll make me pancakes for breakfast!*

She slipped out of bed and pulled on her clothes hurriedly.

'Where are you off to?' grunted Libby, barely looking up.

'Oh, just to see Tan and David,' said Flora, airily, and slid past the table.

Libby reached the end of her paragraph before she stopped to look at her watch.

'Flora, it's only just past seven o'clock!' she exclaimed.

But Flora had gone.

It was deliciously peaceful on the tow-path. The holiday-makers in the touring narrow boats were still fast asleep and Flora strolled along, feeling superior. It was tempting to wake them all up with a piercing blast on a piece of grass stretched between fingers and thumbs, but she decided not to risk it.

As Buxton Tunnel came into sight, Flora wondered, not for the first time, if there really had been someone with Joss that day a few weeks ago. She had been so sure at the time and had worried about it for days afterwards. She had even gone back to the same spot to see how dark and shadowy it was under the arch.

She stared at it now. It did seem particularly black this morning, in contrast with the bright September light. She couldn't even see the tow-path on her side of the canal. Anyone or anything could be hiding in the silent darkness.

Just then, uncannily clear in the still air, Flora heard voices. The next moment a cold shiver of horror ran down her, as a young man—there was no mistake this time—stepped out of the tunnel into full view on the tow-path. He was big and looked angry, but that was all Flora saw before he suddenly disappeared, just as if someone had yanked him back.

Joss! thought Flora. *I'm sure it's Joss.*

Her heart pounding and her mouth suddenly dry, Flora crept nearer. She felt a desperate urge to flatten herself against something, but all around there was nothing but open fields until the rhododendrons of Buxton House. If Joss was meeting someone secretly, Flora could see why she chose the shadows of Buxton Tunnel.

On tiptoe, Flora scurried for the cover of the rhododendrons. She could hear the voices perfectly clearly now.

'So that's it for now, right! I've got nothing else left! Got it? NOTHING ELSE LEFT!' That was Joss, Flora was sure of it.

The other voice was low and menacing. 'Well, think of something else then, all right? Use that brain everyone's so proud of!'

'Oh, get stuffed!' retorted the first voice. Then, and with no warning at all, so that Flora didn't even have time to flatten herself further into the bushes, Joss stalked out from the shadows.

She spotted Flora straightaway. Flora was trapped, clearly visible, and all too obviously trying not to be. For an instant, a look of panic flashed across Joss' face, but the next moment it was replaced by one of scornful fury.

'You!' she almost spat. 'Spying on me. I might have

guessed you'd do something sneaky like that.'

Flora gulped. She was so shaken, she could think of nothing to say.

'I was—I was only…' she stammered, feebly.

'Oh, don't bother to try and think up some pathetic excuse,' Joss snapped. 'Just keep quiet, that's all. You haven't seen anything, all right? Got that?'

Flora nodded dumbly. Her legs were shaking and she wanted to cry. What had happened to Joss? What had her meetings with the strange young man done to her? She might as well be a different person from the one who had written all Flora's excuse notes.

'Good,' said Joss, briskly, beginning to walk away, 'because you just remember that whatever you know about me, I know a lot more about you, OK?'

'If you tell about me, I'll tell about you,' retorted Flora, but in a voice which trembled. She felt stupid and angry and terrified all at the same time. Joss had been right that day; she *was* a wimp.

'Ah, but I won't say a word so long as you just keep your mouth shut,' sneered Joss over her shoulder and then she ran off down the tow-path.

Flora slumped down in the dirt. She was shaking all over and felt sick. All she wanted to do was run into Buxton House and pour it all out to Tan and David. But she daren't; she mustn't. Whatever Joss was up to, she simply *couldn't* risk telling anyone.

But what was it all about? It clearly wasn't just the boat yard, or even the row with Flora. What had Joss meant—*I've got nothing else left?* She'd sounded angry, but also frightened. Who was the strange man and what was the hold he had over Joss? With a jolt of fear, Flora realized that whoever he was and whatever he was doing there, he probably wasn't very far away. Without another thought, Flora leaped to her feet and ran back to the *Thorpe Cloud* as fast as her trembling legs would carry her.

13

The new school year started late for Flora. Her meeting with Joss had been followed by a migraine attack.

'Oh, Flora,' sighed Libby, as she spooned out her medicine. 'This isn't a very good way to start the year, is it? And you've been quite a lot better over the summer, too. I really thought the new diet was working.'

Flora said nothing. She thought it was too. But this migraine was because of Joss.

On the day when she was despatched to Buxton House to complete her recovery—Libby didn't stop to think about it now—Flora was longing to get a moment alone with Tan. He had developed a sudden interest in lifeboats, thanks to a visit they had made to a lifeboat station on a trip to the seaside and it seemed a very long morning that they spent trying to build models of self-righting boats. Flora couldn't quite let go and enjoy herself as she had before the holidays. She was too worried about Joss. She knew deep down that she ought to tell someone what she had seen—Joss might be in real danger—but she simply couldn't bring herself to do it. Time and again she told herself it wasn't any of her business and, anyway, Joss had *told* her not to say anything, but it still kept gnawing away at her conscience. Meanwhile, however, there were more immediate problems to solve.

'Tan, what am I going to do about my bus pass?' she wailed, as soon as they were alone in the den. 'They change colour every year. It'll be obvious that mine's out of date!'

'Crikey,' said Tan. 'I'd completely forgotten about that.'

'I know. So had I.'

They sat in silence for several minutes, racking their brains.

'Got it!' Tan announced, suddenly. 'We must be really dense not to have realized before!'

'Realized what?'

'Don't you see? You don't even need a bus pass any more!'

'Why not? I don't get it,' said Flora.

'Well, the only reason you had to catch the bus was because you couldn't tell Joss what we were doing and ask her to cover for you. How were we supposed to know she'd work it out herself and decide to keep quiet? But seeing as she does know, all you need to do is just come round through the fields to our house every morning. Easy!'

Flora looked unhappy. 'But what if she suddenly decides to tell?'

'Well, there's nothing we can do about that,' said Tan, reasonably. 'Just pray that she doesn't. And, anyway, why should she? She hasn't split on you so far. Why should she change her mind now?'

Flora pulled a face. Tan was always such an optimist. And then, suddenly thrown up in her mind's eye, there was a picture of herself, trembling on the tow-path before a sneering Joss.

If you tell about me, I'll tell about you, Flora had

said, looking like a scared rabbit. At the time she had felt like a wimp but now it seemed like the most sensible thing she could have said.

She smiled slowly. 'No,' she said quietly. 'Joss won't suddenly change her mind. I'm sure of it.'

The next day Flora set out for the bus-stop, just as she had before the summer holidays. Instead of stopping, however, she walked past it and on to where a footpath crossed the fields. She knew from her long tramps with Libby that before long it joined the track which led to Buxton Tunnel. This was the dangerous bit. It was early enough in the morning for the village to be quiet, but the path was popular with dog walkers. Perhaps it would be as well to hide in the undergrowth for a while. Nonetheless, Flora couldn't help a backward glance to see how Joss was taking it.

She was standing, open-mouthed at the bus-stop.

'Bye, Joss,' Flora called, hardly believing her daring. 'You won't say anything now, will you?'

And Flora knew from Joss' furious glare that she had heard and understood. Perfectly.

Stanley Hobbs, Educational Welfare Officer, was sorting out his files. It was always useful to do it just after the start of the term. Some children would have moved away and some new ones would have arrived. Nothing was ever definite for the first few days. He was just about to add a folder to his ever-growing pile of rubbish when he hesitated. *Flora Adams*. Hmm. He wasn't sure he wanted to throw that one away just yet. He sat down and opened it thoughtfully. What had the last letter said? That her new school hadn't been decided yet? He glanced through it again quickly. Yes, that was right—and there had been no other letters since then, or none that had reached the file. He would have to check with her old school. It was probably nothing to worry about. The chances were that Flora was happily settling into her new school and her mother had simply forgotten to send on the address. Flora's records had to be forwarded, though and—well, it was better to be safe than sorry. You couldn't let a child disappear from school and not be very sure where she had ended up—not in this day and age.

Flora quickly settled into a new pattern. She left the *Thorpe Cloud* as if for the bus each day, lurked for a few moments by the bus-stop and then, as soon as she was sure there was no one around to see her, she scurried along to the footpath. Constantly on the lookout for dog walkers, she furtively made her way to Buxton House. It was a tense business and she was nearly rumbled on several occasions. One morning, with plenty of time to hide in the over-ripe oilseed rape, she spotted a very tall man from a neighbouring boat. She threw herself in amongst the damp vegetation and crouched low. It smelt rank but she was sure she was safe. But she had forgotten the man's little Jack Russell, who bounded ahead and delightedly followed her into her hide-out, yapping and waggling his small, stubby tail in greeting.

'*Go away*!' Flora hissed, pushing the little dog back as best she could. He, of course, thought it was a game and yapped the louder.

'Caspar! Here, boy! What are you doing, you tinker? Found a rabbit?'

Flora could see the man's legs and feet only a metre

or so from her own. Any moment now she'd be discovered, she was certain.

Please God, she prayed, desperately, *I know I'm a wimp and you'd probably call me a liar too—but it is all in a good cause—so PLEASE don't let that man find me. PLEASE!*

She froze, willing the dog to go. To her amazement, he gave another half-hearted sniff at her and then trotted out obediently onto the footpath. The next moment both dog and owner had gone.

Flora gave such a huge sigh of relief that a little vole, already terrified by all the commotion, shot out across the footpath in sheer panic. Flora picked herself up, peered out across the top of the oilseed rape and then continued her journey, brushing herself down as she walked, screwing up her nose at the awful, acrid smell which lingered on her clothing.

For the first time she seriously questioned what she was doing. It had been exciting for a few days, but the constant worry about being caught, not to mention the occasional need to dive for cover, was beginning to distress her. What would she do when all the crops were harvested and the fields were naked and open? And, although she would never have admitted it to Tan, now that she didn't spend half the morning walking back from school, the time on her own in the den was beginning to feel a bit long. For a brief moment—and she pushed the thought away immediately, feeling like a traitor—she wondered if school would be quite as bad, now that she could read and her writing was so much better.

She was still deep in thought when she reached Buxton House and pushed open the den door, so it took her a moment to realize that there was someone else there.

Tan must have been hovering right by the door, waiting for her. He grabbed her by the arms and pulled her in.

'Flora, I'm sorry, I'm so sorry,' he blurted out. 'I didn't tell him—he found out for himself somehow. You've got to believe me, Flora! Please!'

'Who? What?' said Flora, in a dazed voice. It was dark in the den and her eyes were slow to adjust after the bright September light. Nevertheless, it was obvious that Tan had been crying.

The armchair creaked and Flora peered past Tan. They were not alone.

'Good morning, Flora,' said David.

14

'How did you find out?'

Flora said the first thing that came into her head. She was too shocked to think further than that. Yet.

'It was easy really, Flora,' David said in a very neutral voice. 'For weeks before the holiday Tan became very keen to leave what he was doing at lunchtime and rush off down to his den—every day. He'd never been such a clock-watcher before. If he was in the middle of doing something he'd just come back and carry on with it after lunch. But not any more. At first I thought he had some secret project going on in the den, especially as he grew very loathe to leave the house to go on outings, or even to have other kids round, but time went by and nothing emerged. He never needed special materials or any help from me. Then the school holidays started and suddenly he was back to normal. Of course, I didn't think anything of it at the time, but when he started clock-watching again a couple of weeks ago, I began to put two and two together.'

'I'm so sorry, Flora,' Tan groaned. 'It's all my fault. I should have realized what I was doing.'

'It's all right,' said Flora, distractedly. 'I should have realized too.'

She sat down heavily. Now that the prospect of being sent back to school suddenly loomed before her, she knew that, however boring her mornings in the den might get, nothing could compare with the awfulness of school. Not for everyone, of course. It worked brilliantly for heaps of people. After all, Joss had always loved it. But it didn't work for Flora. Most definitely not. She felt weak at the knees.

She could feel David watching her and hated him. Oh, he worked very hard at being nice to her. Of course he did. He wanted Libby. It was important to admit that now. Because she wasn't going to cry and beg for mercy. She wasn't going to be a wimp. No. She was going to fight. And she had to know what her weapons were.

'Why today?' she demanded. 'Why go and spoil it all today? Why not last week? Or next week?'

'I saw you,' said David, simply. 'Before that it was all only suspicion.'

'Where? In the village? On the path by the bus-stop?'

David laughed ruefully. 'Oh no, Flora. You were much closer to home than that. I saw you hurrying across the lawn yesterday morning.'

'You were spying!'

'No, Flora, I wasn't. You won't believe me, but I didn't really want to find out. I was hoping there was some other explanation. I was opening the window in my studio and there you were.'

'So now you've gone and spoilt it all!'

David looked at her very seriously. 'I've spent a long time thinking about it, Flora. Hours, actually.'

'Huh!' Flora squeezed her eyes tight and clenched her fists to keep back the tears. Why did he have to be so *nice* about it? Stupid! She knew, didn't she? Libby! But knowing didn't make it any easier to deal with. Flora longed for everything to be all right between them again. She remembered the way he had carried her to the *Thorpe Cloud*, cradled protectively against his chest, the very first day she had met him. It didn't help.

Tan moaned slightly, like a small animal in pain. He was huddled up on the desk seat, his arms about his head. Flora knew he felt as bad as she did, probably worse, and it gave her strength.

'I suppose you'll say you've *prayed* about it?' she spat at David.

'Yes,' David agreed.

'And God thinks I should go back to school, does he? Even though my eczema's getting better and I've had hardly any migraines? Even though I can read now and I'm learning much more? God's on *your* side, is he? God's with the grown-ups?'

'I never said I thought you should go back to school, Flora,' said David, gently. 'But God, I expect, is on the side of the truth.'

'Oh.' Flora blushed scarlet. He had all the best shots. She was overwhelmed by a terrible sense of shame. Ashamed of hating David, ashamed of being so mean about Libby, ashamed of hitting Joss—but most of all ashamed of the great web of lies she and Tan had built up.

But she couldn't admit it. Not any of it. Not to David. If she said another word, she would burst out crying and howl like a baby. No, no, *no*. She wasn't a wimp or a scabby little drip. No matter what he said, or how nicely he said it, David was the enemy. He had proved he was. Why had he said anything at all if he didn't think she should go back to school? He was trying to make her think he was on her side. *He* was lying. He must be!

'Aagh!' she burst out, and slammed her tight fists so

hard against the wall that she scuffed some skin off her knuckles. Then she leaped up, opened the door and ran.

She had nowhere to go, of course. She couldn't go home because she was supposed to be at school and she could hardly go and hide in Buxton House. She stood on the tow-path fretfully. Somewhere to cry, that's what she needed. Somewhere private to go and howl.

In the tunnel. That's where she'd go. This morning the arch of darkness looked velvety and welcoming. There was no one about and anyway, she hadn't much choice. She darted underneath and collapsed in the damp earth, unable to restrain her tears any longer.

She cried for a long time, her sobs echoing eerily in the enclosed space. So what if anyone heard her? The game was up now anyway, wasn't it?

Flora jumped violently when a hand touched her shoulder. She hadn't heard anyone approach.

'Flora! Stop it. Please. I can't bear it.'

It was Tan.

'Leave me alone,' Flora sobbed. 'There's nothing you can do. Just leave me alone.'

'But I can't leave you crying like that. Please, Flora. Dad's gone back to the house, now. Come with me to the den till you feel better.'

'I'll *never* feel better,' Flora raged. 'And I never want to see that den again. Just leave me alone, will you? Go away and leave me alone! I mean it!'

Sadly, Tan backed away and turned to go. Even several metres away from the tunnel, he could hear Flora's terrible, raw crying, amplified by the arch. He couldn't just go and leave her, so he sat down on the tow-path and buried his head between his knees.

What a mess! he thought despairingly, pressing his sore eyes against his kneecaps. He couldn't think what on earth they were going to do. He knew from the uncomfortable interview early that morning that his father thought he had been wrong to help Flora, whatever good had come from it.

'I thought I could rely on you to be honest,' David had said, looking him straight in the eye, 'and instead you've helped Flora to deceive me, to deceive her school and even to deceive her own mother.'

'But her mum doesn't want her mixing with a load of kids who call her names!' Tan had protested, lamely.

'Nor does she want her to be educated out of school. You know because I've told you. Don't pretend. Whatever Libby said about name-calling was just a chance remark she made when she was angry and upset. And you knew that too. I had thought better of you, Tan.'

Tan had squirmed miserably. He knew, all right. He'd known all along. But he'd wanted to help Flora. And, if he was really honest with himself, he had wanted the excitement of a new project—a really big one.

Now, sitting in the dirt on the tow-path, blinking back tears, he knew he'd gone the wrong way about it. But how did that help? They couldn't send Flora back to school—they couldn't. It would be too cruel. Poor, poor, Flora. What a mess he had made!

O God, God, God! I never meant it to be like this! he shouted in his head. *Just get us out of this mess! Please!*

15

Flora stopped sobbing. Through the awful howling, which somehow didn't seem to have much to do with her, she had gradually become aware of the steady chug-chug of an approaching narrow boat. It didn't matter if anyone saw her out of school during school hours—not any more—but she didn't want curious looks or sympathetic questions. She picked herself up quickly and flattened herself against the brickwork, hoping the crew wouldn't notice her in the dark and praying that there wasn't a dog on board.

Luckily, the crew were far more concerned with steering their boat through the narrow cut than about anyone who might be lurking on the tow-path, and there was no sign of a dog.

Flora breathed a sigh of relief and sat down again. She didn't want to stay there much longer. Now that she'd stopped crying, she was exhausted and hungry. It was chilly in the tunnel, despite the bright day, and she'd also remembered Joss' strange man. She didn't feel very safe, all alone in the dark. Libby would have thrown a fit if she'd known.

But where could she go? She couldn't face going back to the *Thorpe Cloud* and explaining everything to Libby. Perhaps she could go to Zilla and hide on board the *Argo*? No. The thought of Zilla telling Joss was unbearable.

105

But she must eat something soon. If she didn't, she'd get a migraine and she didn't want that on top of all this. Or did she? A day of obliterating pain almost seemed like a good escape.

Footsteps. Flora's heart began to pound and her mouth went dry. They were too heavy to be Tan's. *Don't be silly*, she told herself. *Loads of people walk along here. It doesn't have to be Joss' man.*

She could hear low voices coming from outside the tunnel and then…

'Flora?' It was David. Flora didn't know whether to be relieved or not. 'Flora, I know you don't want to, but you're going to have to talk to me.'

Flora said nothing. She could hear the footsteps coming closer, inside the archway now. Well, she could run but what was the point? And she was worn out. But she didn't have to co-operate with him, did she?

She could see him now, colourless in the gloom. She knew he wouldn't have spotted her yet. His eyes would have to get used to the dark. It made her feel pleasingly powerful, just for a moment or two.

'I'm here,' she said, before David fell over her, and she had the satisfaction of seeing him jump.

'I've brought you something to eat,' he said.

Flora didn't respond. Why, oh why did he always have to be so *kind*? She must keep in mind that he was the enemy.

'For goodness' sake, take it, Flora,' said David, for once sounding exasperated. 'I haven't poisoned it, you know. I just want to spare you some pain!'

'Hah!' snorted Flora. 'Nice of you to think about me and how I feel!'

'Of course I think about how you feel, Flora.' He

sounded tired. 'What do you take me for? An ogre? D'you think I've enjoyed this morning?'

'Well, why didn't you just keep quiet?' demanded Flora. 'We were quite happy! And we weren't doing anything wrong—well, nothing against the law, anyway!'

David sighed. 'Can I sit down, please?' he said.

Flora grunted.

'Put yourself in my place, Flora. What d'you think it's like for me? I find out that my son is helping his best friend to deceive her mother and the Local Education Authority—on my property! That alone puts me in a very difficult position. And, as if that weren't enough, his best friend happens to be the daughter of the woman I've fallen in love with.'

Flora gave a strangled gasp.

'Yes, I'm not ashamed to admit it and I know you don't like it, but that's the way it is, OK?'

Flora said nothing. Of course it wasn't OK. What did he expect her to say? Her head was pounding so hard that it was difficult to concentrate on what he was saying. Oh, she had known—she had known for ages now—but hearing David say it made it unavoidable and concrete. She felt stunned.

'So what am I to do? Where should my loyalties lie?' David's voice seemed to be coming from a long way off and Flora had to struggle to make sense of what he said.

'Should I support my son, who I can see is trying to do something good?' David continued. 'And his best friend, who is suddenly so much happier? But that means helping them lie to the woman I love. And to everyone else who has anything to do with them.'

David paused and Flora could feel him looking sideways at her, trying to meet her eyes through the gloom.

She shut them tight and clenched her fists.

'It isn't easy for me either, Flora. I don't want you to be hurt. And I have to ask myself, what does God think of all this? Because God is probably more important than anything else in my life. And God, after all, is love.'

'Love?' snapped Flora, blindly. 'If you really loved Tan, you'd do what *he* wanted. But you love my mum better than him now, so you're doing what *she* wants!'

'Flora, it isn't like that. I haven't run out of love for Tan because I love Libby. I've got enough love for them both.'

'Well, I can tell where *I'm* going to come out of all this,' said Flora, bitterly. 'Right at the bottom!'

David heaved a sigh and passed a hand across his brow, in the very same gesture Tan used when he was beat. Flora winced.

'I'm not doing this very well, am I?' he said.

Flora said nothing.

'OK, I'll try again. Let's be dead clear about this, because this is what I've decided and I'm not going to change my mind.'

Flora sat up straighter. His tone had changed. He was suddenly brisk and business-like.

'As far as I'm concerned, what you and Tan are doing is wrong. But if I go and tell Libby, neither of you will ever forgive me. I know what *I* think we should do, but you and Tan don't agree. Well, I can't force you to think I'm right and I care about your opinion.'

'I don't understand,' said Flora, fiercely. 'What are you going to do?'

'Nothing. Well, not yet, anyway. It's up to you. It's your lie.'

'Oh,' said Flora. She sat in silence for a moment,

wondering why she didn't feel any sense of relief. *It's OK!* she told herself. *He's not going to tell anyone. I don't have to go back to school!*

But for some reason that she didn't understand, she felt strangely flat and alone. Not relieved. Just cold and tired and empty. And anyway…

'Not yet?' she said, her voice shaking. 'You said, "Not yet." How long have I got?'

'A week.' David was very clear and calm. 'I can't leave it any longer than that. You've got till next Tuesday to sort this out with Libby. After that, I'll have no choice but to tell her.'

David reached out and patted her knee, but she flinched away as if his touch burned. 'I'm sorry, love,' he said, gently. 'Let me know if you need any help. And, for pity's sake, eat these.' He stood up stiffly and dropped a large bag of sandwiches into her lap.

Stanley Hobbs toyed with the folder in his hands. Still there had been no word from Flora Adams' mother. It was time to do something about it. He picked up a pen.

Dear Ms Adams, he began.

It has now been some time since we heard from you about your plans for the schooling of your daughter, Flora, and her previous school is anxious to know where her records should be sent.

He sat back and considered. He was sure it would be all right—but you just never knew. An anxious child who struggled with her schoolwork and was frequently absent? Just what *was* going on at home? Yes, he would send the letter. He had left it long enough.

16

Once again Flora lay huddled up in her bunk. She couldn't sleep. It had been the most miserable day she could ever remember. She had eaten David's sandwiches, hating him through every mouthful, so she hadn't got a migraine—but her head ached with bad temper and despair. She had spent a long time in the tunnel, fretting, and she had scratched one wrist raw, just out of worry and long habit.

Now she hated herself. She had been foul to Tan, who, once David was out of the way, had kept a silent vigil outside the tunnel, broken only by his sporadic attempts to get her out. It had been the afternoon before she had finally given in, shamed by his persistence.

'I brought you these,' he had said, handing her an almost identical package to the one his father had brought her that morning.

'Oh, you're as bad as him!' she had stormed, snatching up the sandwiches and flinging them into the canal. Then she had burst into tears.

Tan, with a long-suffering gentleness so like his father's that, for Flora, it was like sandpaper on a wound, had found her a hankie. Then he had coaxed her back to the den and gone off in search of more food. When he'd returned, he had tried to jolly her out of her black mood, telling her time and again that they were bound to come up with something. Finally, he had lost patience with her, called her a few rude names and stomped off to the house. It had been a long time before Flora could face picking herself up and making her way home, cross, weary and more lonely than she had ever been in her entire life.

Libby had taken one look at her and sent her to bed with a dose of medicine inside her. Flora didn't bother to argue. What did it matter, anyway? What did anything matter any more? Everything she ever did turned out to be a disaster. She should have known that leaving school would never work. Because it wasn't just school, was it? Millions of other kids went to school and loved it. It was her, Flora. She couldn't do anything properly. She couldn't cope with school, she couldn't keep her friends, she couldn't even get herself to the den each morning without being seen. She was useless at everything. A complete drip.

Flora lay awake in the dark for what seemed like hours, listening to the steady thumpety-thump of Libby's typewriter. Suddenly there was a quiet tap on the *Thorpe Cloud*'s door.

Flora's heart thudded frighteningly fast and she curled up in a tight ball, her duvet clutched around her. David! It must be! He had changed his mind and come to tell Libby!

Please God, no! she begged silently. It was worth a try. *I know I'm useless but...*

It wasn't David. It was Zilla. What on earth could she want?

Immediately, Flora knew. Joss must have told her. Why today of all days, Flora had no idea, but that must be it. Joss had told Zilla that Flora wasn't going to school and Zilla had pondered all evening about how she would break the news to Libby.

Flora lay braced to hear the fatal words for a long time. She could hear the sounds of the kettle being put on to boil and mugs and biscuits being found, and then the shuffling of Libby's papers as she tidied away. All the while, the two women talked quietly about this and that—but surely Zilla couldn't have come round just for a chat? Not at this time of night? The suspense was unbearable. Flora wondered if she should rush out in her pyjamas and confess everything straightaway.

Just as she had decided that she could bear it no longer, Flora heard the words she'd been waiting for.

'Well, Libby, I'm sorry to be a nuisance but I *really* came round here to...'

A dull roaring seemed to fill Flora's ears. This was it. The moment had come. She wanted to leap out of bed and scream at Zilla not to tell because it *did* still matter. She could make it up with Tan. They could think of something, she knew they could. She would *prove* that she could do something right. And, for her, not going to school *was* right. She knew it was. If only, by some miracle, Zilla didn't tell!

Flora propped herself up on an elbow and strained to hear what was being said.

'Oh no!' said Libby. It didn't sound promising.

'Yes, it's been going on for some time now, I'm afraid. I've lost track of how long.'

A silent tear rolled down Flora's face. Seconds now and she would be dragged out of bed to face Libby's wrath.

'I would have told you sooner, but it took us a long

time to work out what was going on,' continued Zilla. 'To be honest, at first we thought we must be imagining things.'

Why hadn't Libby stormed in to get her? It wasn't like her to keep her anger to herself. She must be stunned— so shocked and angry that she couldn't move. It was terrifying. Flora couldn't bear to think how furious she would be when she did finally come for her. Maybe she would wait till Zilla had gone? Oh no! That would be even worse!

Flora pulled the duvet over her ears.

'Please, God,' she whispered. 'Please help me.'

If only David were here. He had such a calming effect on Libby. If only she had let *him* tell her. That would have been so much easier than this. And he would have defended her. He would have told Libby all the good things about what she and Tan had done. She knew that now. Oh, why had she been so nasty to him? Why hadn't she let him tell Libby straightaway?

Still Libby didn't come. Maybe she didn't want to say anything in front of Zilla. Worse, maybe she wasn't going to say anything till morning. Flora couldn't bear it. She'd rather face it now.

With fierce determination, Flora threw back her duvet and padded across into the living area.

Libby and Zilla looked up in surprise.

'Mum, I…' Flora stammered and then couldn't get any further.

'Flora, love, I'm sorry. Did we disturb you? We were trying to be very quiet,' said Libby, apologetically.

Funny, thought Flora. *She doesn't look angry. Worried, yes, but not angry.*

'I'm sorry, Flora,' said Zilla, kindly. 'I just came round

to tell your mum something and to ask her advice.'

'What about?' croaked Flora, dazed.

The two women looked at each other.

'Oh, it was just…' Libby stopped, unsure whether to go on.

'I think we might as well tell her,' said Zilla, consideringly. 'You never know, Libby. She might be able to help.'

Flora sat rigid and upright on the small armchair Zilla had vacated for her, a mug of untouched Horlicks at her side. Zilla hadn't come to tell Libby about Flora. No. She had come for advice about something else. Something which, in many ways, was much worse.

Things had been going missing from the *Argo*. Just little things at first, the sort of things you wouldn't notice until you got the feeling that you were mislaying too many handfuls of change or odd pound coins. And then it was bigger things. An expensive bottle of wine which they'd been saving for a special occasion. An ornament that nobody liked but everyone knew was rare and valuable. Torches—goodness, they were always losing torches but *this* many? And then there was Joss' room. Zilla didn't go in very often. It was up to Joss to clean it and her parents had always believed in respecting their children's privacy—but Zilla was sure there weren't so many knick-knacks lying around. There was one particular candleholder that Joss had been given by a great-aunt—it was an ugly thing but made of antique silver—where was that?

And now, today, they had had this terrible scene with Joss. Joss had started it, of course. She was so badtempered and unlike herself these days. They had put it down to her age and worrying about the boat yard at first. Then they had blamed it on starting a new school.

But now they were wondering if there was something else.

Reuben had been going through the band's bookings over their evening meal. It was a busy time of the year for them—lots of hoedowns and harvest suppers to play at.

'It'd be good if we could hear more of your flute, Joss,' Reuben had said, encouragingly.

'She hasn't played it for weeks,' Zilla explained to Flora. 'She keeps saying she doesn't feel like it. Well, that's understandable. It's not easy to stand up and play in front of a crowd of strangers and, the age she is, we just thought she was self-conscious. But then we began to realize she wasn't even practising on her own.'

Flora nodded. She'd noticed too, of course. She sat, poised on the edge of her chair, her fists clenched. A terrible suspicion was beginning to dawn in her mind.

'Well, we talked it through, Reuben and I, and decided to say nothing. I mean, the last thing we wanted was for it to become a big issue. If she wanted to take a break from her flute and the band, then we should let her. Live and let live, that's what I say. But Reuben, well, he's taken it harder and, I suppose, since we were talking about the band anyway, well, he couldn't resist just *mentioning* it. That's all he did. He only *mentioned* it.

'What happened?' asked Flora, fairly sure that she could guess.

'Well, you wouldn't believe it. Joss just flew off the handle. This great flood of abuse about how we were exploiting her and we ought to be paying her a proper fee for the bookings and how it was interfering with her school work and goodness knows what! She was like a different child from the one who was begging to be allowed to play at a function only a year ago.'

Flora nodded. She knew that feeling only too well.

'Reuben stayed very calm, of course. I must admit, I felt like boxing her ears but Reuben is a patient man. He carefully explained to her that we couldn't pay her until she was older because of the laws about child employment. Anyway, at the moment she isn't really a full member of the band—more of a kind of apprentice.'

'But you *do* pay her,' protested Flora. 'She's told me.'

'Oh, we give her a share of the tips—that's only fair—but we don't pay her a proper fee. And she's always been happy with that—delighted, in fact. Until now.'

'Which is really odd because she isn't actually playing in the band at the moment,' put in Libby, who had been listening intently, although she knew the gist of the story. 'Hasn't been for weeks.'

'No, and now she says she won't. Not unless we pay her properly. Which she must know won't happen. So what is the child up to?'

'Could it really be because she's worried about her homework?' asked Libby, tentatively. 'I suppose she gets quite a lot, now she's at secondary school.'

Zilla just looked at her. Flora felt sick. It would be nice to think it was all about homework. That would be simple enough. But they all knew it wasn't. Not with so many things going missing from the *Argo* as well. No. Something far more sinister was going on.

17

'You're up early,' said Libby the next morning, stopping typing in surprise. 'I thought after such a disturbed night, you'd want to lie in for as long as possible. Are you sure you don't want to go back for a while? You look exhausted.'

'I can't sleep,' said Flora, miserably. 'I'm so worried about Joss.'

It was about half the truth. In fact, she had spent the night wrestling with her conscience. She ought to say something about the strange young man. Of course she should. Obviously he had something to do with Joss' behaviour. There were all sorts of awful possibilities. But then there would be the waiting. The waiting whilst Libby told Zilla and Zilla told Reuben. Then more waiting whilst they hummed and hawed and decided what to do. In the end, they would speak to Joss and then Joss would tell about Flora and Tan. No. She couldn't do it. Better to be upfront about it and admit everything immediately.

It was easier said than done. Late at night, faced with the thought of Joss telling, Flora had been prepared to come clean. But not any more. The heat of the moment had passed and, as the morning approached, the chill in Flora's heart increased. Tell Libby? Just like that? Over breakfast? No. She couldn't face that either.

It would mean school. There was no doubt about it. And, even though she could read properly and write much better now, everything else would be the same—the noise and the heat and the teachers. And, worst of all, the kids. How they would scoff at her when they knew what she had done! She had one week. One week to work something out.

All through the long, early morning hours, Flora had struggled to find a way through, but when she finally blundered into the living area in search of breakfast, she was no nearer a solution.

'I'll make you some tea,' said Libby and Flora realized how dreadful she must look. It was so unlike Libby to take a break from her work for anything.

'No, it's OK,' she protested. 'I can do it myself. You've got work to do.'

'I can stop for a minute,' said Libby, firmly. 'Sit down. You'll be having a migraine if you're not careful.'

Flora did as she was told and tried to look cheerful. She was very aware that Libby was watching her carefully.

'Try not to worry yourself sick about Joss,' she said. 'I know she used to be your best friend but there really isn't any point in worrying. There's nothing you can do. It's up to Reuben and Zilla. They've brought up four other children, so they ought to have some idea how to handle it.'

'Four?' said Flora, blearily. 'I can only think of three.'

'Oh, Flora, you're still half asleep. You're forgetting…'

At that moment, there was a thump on the *Thorpe Cloud*'s door and Tan bounded in.

'Hi, Libby,' he said, breezily. 'Sorry to bother you so early. Can I talk to Flora, please?'

Tan. What on earth was she to say to Tan after yesterday? It all seemed so long ago, and yet the awfulness of her behaviour suddenly hit her with the force of a head-butt in the stomach. But what had Libby been saying just before he came in? Flora had that strange tugging feeling you get in your brain when you want to catch hold of a thought because it's important.

'Fire away,' said Libby casually to Tan.

'No, I meant in private, actually,' he replied. 'She'll have to get dressed.'

'Tan! Can't it wait? Flora hasn't even had breakfast yet and, actually, I was thinking of sending her back to bed, she looks so ill.'

'Ah, well, that's why I want to talk to her,' said Tan, somewhat awkwardly. 'I was pretty horrible to her yesterday—enough to make anyone ill.'

'*You* were horrible to *me*?' Flora gasped. 'How can you say that? It was me that was horrible to you!'

'Well, I called you a... '

'Thank you!' interrupted Libby, quickly. 'I don't think I want to hear all the gory details. If that's the way it is, Tan's right. You'd better go away and finish this conversation somewhere else. Get your clothes on quickly, Flora.'

'She can have breakfast at my house,' Tan offered.

'Fine,' agreed Libby. 'Just take her away and sort yourselves out.'

Flora threw on her clothes and moments later was out on the tow-path with Tan, leaving Libby to get back to work with an amused smile on her face.

'I'm sorry,' said Tan, as soon as they were out of earshot of the *Thorpe Cloud*. 'I should never have gone and left you in the den like that. And I didn't mean any

119

of those things I called you. I was just fed up.'

Flora didn't say anything. She couldn't, there was such a hard lump in her throat.

'Flora? It is all right, isn't it? I mean, you'll still be my friend? I worried about you all night. I mean, the mood you were in, you might have jumped in the canal or anything.'

Now he came to mention it, Flora could see that he must be as tired as she was. In his brown face, the shadows under his eyes were almost maroon.

'Oh, stop being so *nice*!' she burst out. 'It's me that should be saying sorry. I was horrible to you *all day*!'

And, with that, she fell to hammering her fists in the dirt of the tow-path and sobbing.

'Oh crikey,' said Tan.

That afternoon, at around three o'clock, a nervous Tan arrived at the den with a plate of sandwiches and a huge mug of tea. He hoped Flora would be all right by now. When she had stopped howling that morning, they had hidden in the den and he had gone off to get some breakfast. She had refused to go to the house herself because she couldn't face David. Then they had had to go through the farce of Flora going back to the *Thorpe Cloud* and persuading Libby that she was fit to go to school before she actually returned to the den. Neither of them could think what else to do.

Tan spent a miserably awkward day with David.

'Is she in the den, then?' David had asked coolly, when Tan was ready to start work.

'I should think so,' Tan muttered, desperately hoping that she had got back safely. She had looked dreadful. He didn't speak to his father again until half past twelve.

'I'd better go and check she's all right,' said Tan, apologetically. He had thought of little else all morning.

David, his mind on his work, nodded briefly and Tan scurried off to find Flora curled up in the armchair, fast asleep. She looked exhausted. Tan dragged a duvet down from the house to cover her up and then left her.

At half past one, she was still fast asleep. And at half past two.

At three o' clock, a sudden awful thought struck Tan.

'She hasn't had anything to eat,' he wailed, his head jerking up from the drawing he was messing around with. 'I let her sleep through lunch!'

'Oh, for goodness' sake,' said David, irritably. 'That's all we need. Go and get her some food, then.'

When Tan opened the den door, Flora was still asleep. He set down the plate and the mug and shook her gently.

'Flora!' he said. 'It's time to wake up. You've got to eat something. Come on! Wake up!'

Flora opened her eyes, worked out where she was, saw the sandwiches and almost began to cry.

But she didn't. For one thing she was fed up with looking like a wimp. And for another it would hurt too much.

'Migraine,' she whispered, her voice slurred. 'Tan, I've got a migraine.'

Flora remembered the nightmarish walk along the tow-path for the rest of her life. It felt as if it would never end. Every pebble she stepped on seemed to explode like a grenade in her head. Each moored boat appeared to loom close like a towering monster and then shift away to nothing, so that the canal-side was like a precipice. Tan had wanted to get David to drive her home but Flora wouldn't let him.

'He'd… have… to… lie… to… Libby,' she said, painfully. 'No.'

So Tan had to drag her there, stopping every few paces for her to retch at the side of the tow-path. Each step of the way, he bargained with God.

Let me get her home safely and I'll persuade her to tell Libby the truth. Stop it from hurting her so much, and I'll never tell a lie ever again.

All the way he was muttering under his breath, feeling all the time that God couldn't possibly be taking any notice of such pathetic snivellings.

When they got to the *Thorpe Cloud*, Flora stood still.

'Leave… me… here,' she said.

'No,' said Tan. 'I won't.' He knew what was worrying her. Normally he wouldn't be there. She was supposed to have just got off the school bus.

Flora hadn't the energy or the words to fight.

'I'll sort it out,' said Tan, firmly, and bundled her up the gangplank onto the boat.

'I met her by the shop,' he told Libby when he'd got her through the door. *Sorry, God*, he thought, despairingly. Where would this great tangle of lies end?

Libby hardly seemed to notice he was there, as Flora fell into her arms.

'Oh, I *knew* I shouldn't have let her go to school today!' she exclaimed. 'I knew she was too exhausted. How could I have been so stupid?'

She began to hustle Flora off to her bunk but Flora lifted her head and, barely audible, said, 'I've… forgotten… the… post.'

'What was that?' said Libby, too anxious to understand.

But Tan had heard. 'It's all right, Flora,' he assured her. 'I'll get it.' And then he was off, before Libby thought to ask any awkward questions.

Tan read and reread the official-looking letter in his hand.

Dear Ms Adams,

It has now been some time since we heard from you about your plans for the schooling of your daughter, Flora, and her previous school is anxious to know where her records should be sent. I am sure you will understand the importance of her new school being aware of all the relevant information.

I would therefore be extremely grateful if you could notify both her previous school and myself of her new school's address, so that her records may be forwarded and I can update my file.

Thank you for your help in this matter.

Yours sincerely,

Stanley Hobbs

Educational Welfare Officer

So. It had come to this already. Tan was shocked and chilled. He hadn't expected it so soon. Well, he couldn't tell Flora. It was the last thing she needed just now. He would just have to sort it out by himself. He smiled ruefully. He was becoming a very accomplished liar.

18

Perhaps it was her new diet. Perhaps it was because she was better at taking her medicine. Perhaps God was answering her prayers. Whatever the reason, when Flora woke up the next morning, she was better.

She lifted her head incredulously. Just a very slight twinge. She pushed back her duvet and padded over to the loo. A bit fragile, but that was all.

'Mum, I'm better!' she announced, excitedly.

Libby looked up from her work, in disbelief.

'You do look better,' she said, hesitantly, examining her face carefully. 'But don't go counting your chickens before they're hatched. I'm not letting you go to school today, that's for sure. I'd better see if David will have you for the day.'

'Oh no!' exclaimed Flora, all the awfulness of the previous two days suddenly destroying her delight at being well.

'Why on earth not?' asked Libby, amazed. 'You love it at Buxton House. Don't tell me you and Tan didn't make it up yesterday!'

'Oh no, it's not that,' said Flora quickly, frantically searching her brain for an excuse. 'I mean, I just didn't want to put David to any more trouble—I had breakfast there only yesterday, remember?'

'Oh, don't be silly, Flora. He doesn't mind in the least.

He says you're no trouble at all. You just go along and have a nice, restful day enjoying yourself.'

Enjoying myself? thought Flora. *Little does she know.* The idea of spending a whole day at Buxton House with David was appalling. How could she face him after all that had been said? How could she bear being in the same room with him, with his deadline hanging over her? She would crack up!

Thinking very fast, she said, 'Oh, all right then. I'll go. But he doesn't need to come and get me in the car. If you just give me a note for him, I can walk along after breakfast.'

And hide in the den, she was thinking. *He doesn't even need to know I'm there.*

Libby looked at her oddly. 'What's the matter, Flora? Have you had an argument with David, as well?'

'Oh no, it's fine,' said Flora, breezily, wishing her heart would stop pounding so quickly. She needed to be much more careful what she said. 'I was just trying not to cause any trouble.'

'It's no trouble to me to pop down to the shop to phone him and I'm sure it's no trouble to him to come and fetch you,' said Libby, firmly. 'Now have some breakfast and stop fussing.'

It was a very uncomfortable drive round to Buxton House. Tan tried a few bright and breezy comments like, 'Gosh, Flora. It's great that you've got better so quickly,' but the silence that greeted them was so deep, it was almost painful. David wasn't being deliberately quiet—it was just that Flora and Tan normally filled the car with their chatter.

'Can I go to the den, please?' asked Flora stiffly, as soon as she was out of the car.

'Do whatever you think is best, Flora,' said David, coolly, and walked into the house.

The next few days were terrible. Flora spent the school time miserably trying to work in the den but mostly agonizing over what she should do. Libby had told her that Zilla was thinking of going to the doctor about Joss, which showed just how desperate she was. Normally Zilla had herbs to deal with everything, but Joss had refused to take any.

'There's nothing wrong with me!' she had shouted. 'I asked if I could have more money, not herbs!'

'You can understand it, in a way,' Libby had said. 'I mean, it's always possible that it *isn't* Joss who's taken the stuff. But it's all very odd. I mean, why would Joss choose *now* to make such a fuss about her wages? She *knows* they're still not absolutely sure that the boat yard will be saved. She was always such a considerate girl. It's as if she's had a complete personality change—ever since that row you had with her, Flora.'

It was all unbearable for Flora. And there was no let up at the weekend. They saw far too much of David. By Sunday evening she was exhausted with the effort of trying to pretend to Libby that everything was normal, and of not scratching at her eczema which had flared up badly again. Only two days till David's deadline and she and Tan had thought of nothing.

On Monday morning, Flora had had enough. When she got to the den, she sat down, laid her head on the old desk and began to cry.

'Please, God,' she sobbed. 'Please help me. I don't know what to do.'

She cried for a very long time. When she couldn't cry

any more, she stayed where she was for even longer, her hot, wet cheek lying against the cool, smooth wood of the desk. She could smell the old polish which was now waxy under her fingers where her tears had soaked in. Strangely comforted by the ancient, fusty aroma, she dozed.

An hour or more must have passed before she woke up, her neck stiff and her bottom sore. Her cheek felt flattened and cold where it had been pressed against the desk. She stood up stiffly, yawned and looked at her watch. Nearly half past twelve. She ate the sandwiches which Tan had left for her. She wasn't really hungry but she couldn't think what else to do. The day stretched miserably before her. Tan and David had gone to a drama workshop. Flora had watched Tan struggle with his excitement about going and his misery at leaving her behind and had felt awful. David was right. She should confess everything and go back to school. All the joy of her days in the den had evaporated and Tan's fun was being spoilt too. She knew she had changed over the last few months. Perhaps she would cope better with school now? After all, it wasn't a problem for most people.

But the memory of those first wonderful days in the den held her back. She knew she had worked better and learned more in those weeks before the summer holiday. If only there was some way of getting them back.

She sighed, picked up Tan's copy of *A Little Princess* and curled up in the armchair. She would reread her favourite bit. Maybe it would inspire her.

It didn't. Her brain was too fuggy, anxious and tired. Before long she had worried herself back into an uncomfortable sleep.

It wasn't a refreshing sleep. Strange dreams tormented her and the discomfort of being curled up in the chair kept her close to waking. She dreamt that she was ravenously hungry and that she ought to do something about it...

'You'll be ill if you don't eat,' said a kind-faced man with a huge pot of cream for her eczema and he started to spoon the cream into her mouth.

'Uh... Uh...' protested Flora, flailing about to escape him, but the huge, airy kitchen in which she was trapped began to shrink and darken and close in on her, until she knew she was dying for lack of oxygen and because she was choking on the thick cream which filled her mouth.

And then she died. She knew she had died because, even though the room was pitch black, she could see herself lying on a neat little bed, very cold and still, with one of Joss' exotic scarves stretched over her. A terrible howling filled her ears which she thought must be the mourners, except that she recognized the voice as her own.

A bearded man in a long, rough robe, approached the bed.

'Get up, my child,' he said and turned back Joss' scarf to lift the dead Flora's hand.

So that's how Jesus looks! thought Flora, peacefully, suddenly back in her body on the bed. She raised her hand to take his.

She met his eyes and hesitated. Such powerful eyes! And as she watched they were changing. Suddenly, it wasn't Jesus who was holding out his hand to her, but David.

'Don't touch me,' screamed Flora, shrinking back. 'I don't want you. Go away. I'm not your child.'

The man smiled a sad, tired smile and turned away. 'Do whatever you think is best,' he said.

'No, no, no!' howled Flora. 'Come back! Don't leave me on my own!'

But the man had gone...

19

Suddenly, Flora was awake. She leaped out of the arm-chair and flung open the door. She had to have light and she had to have air—in fact, she had to get away from the dark captivity of the den completely.

And then she stopped. What was that?

A sudden cold finger of horror seemed to stir her insides. Was she still in her dream?

'No, no—stop it! Stop it—leave me alone,' she could hear, perfectly clearly, yet faintly.

For a moment, Flora stood by the open den door, unable to move. Then she got a grip on herself.

'Don't be silly,' she said, out loud. 'It's not your dream. It's someone real.'

And she knew, without a shadow of doubt, exactly who it must be. In one bound, she was at the den window and peering out cautiously.

Sure enough, almost directly below her on the tow-path, stood Joss.

Holding her by the forearms, in a grip so hard that Flora could almost feel the bruises, was a big young man with silky, black hair, just like Joss'.

'Stop it, Alex,' she heard Joss protesting. 'You're really hurting me.'

Alex! Of course! Flora sank down in the armchair. How could she have been so blind and stupid? She had worried and worried, but never thought it through clearly. If she had, she must have realized what was so glaringly obvious. That was what had seemed so important when she was talking to Libby about Joss the morning after Zilla had been round.

'They've brought up four other children, so they ought to have some idea how to handle it,' Libby had said.

'Four?' Flora could hear herself replying. 'I can only think of three.'

She had forgotten Alex, Joss' only brother. Of course, she had never met him. He had left the canal years ago but she knew that Joss still missed him.

'I was just a little girl,' Joss had said, on one of the few occasions she had spoken about him, 'but he used to talk to me a lot. He didn't get on with the others. He couldn't play an instrument—well, not like they could—and he hated being cramped up on the boats. He kept on about space and freedom and being his own person. He desperately wanted a car, but he couldn't even afford driving lessons. He used to buy me sweets because Zilla and Reuben wouldn't. You know, too many additives—they said they were bad for me.'

'So where is he now?' Flora had wanted to know. The idea of this wild, sweetie-buying brother had seemed rather appealing.

'Dunno,' said Joss, sadly. 'The last I heard, he was in prison. I've stopped asking. I don't even know if Zilla and Reuben know where he is.'

Well, there was no doubt about where he was now, Flora was sure of it. He was down on the tow-path shaking Joss.

But what was she to do? Alex obviously didn't want

his parents to know he was back and Joss was helping him to stay hidden. But why? Would Joss want her to get help now? Or would it make her absolutely furious? But Alex was hurting her. Surely Flora couldn't ignore that, whatever Joss had said?

'Oh, help!' Flora moaned. 'What am I to do?'

She could still hear the argument clearly through the window.

'Joss, please. I only need a bit more. Don't give up on me now!'

Alex's voice was pleading, but still loud and aggressive. Flora knelt on the chair and peered cautiously out of the window. Joss was writhing in his grip.

'No!' she shouted. 'You keep saying that and it's been weeks and weeks. And there's nothing else left! I've had enough. You'll have to think of something else!'

'Oh, come on, Joss,' said Alex, shaking her. 'Haven't you got friends? There must be something you can do!'

'What? Steal from my friends, you mean? No way! It's one thing taking stuff from your parents to give to your brother but I am not doing *anything* else! I'm not ending up like you! Give me a break, can't you? For God's sake, I even sold my flute!'

Something in Flora's heart cracked. What was she doing standing there, watching Joss' desperate face as she struggled with her brother? It had gone far enough. Joss had sold her *flute*! Flora didn't care how much Joss was trying to protect Alex, she was going to get help! Not because the flute was worth a lot of money—though it was, of course—but because she knew how much it had meant to Joss. It must have torn her apart to sell it.

Breathless with horror, Flora raced along the path

towards the house. Her eyes smarted with tears. Poor Joss! It wasn't surprising she had been behaving so oddly and all the time Flora had done nothing.

Smack! Flora staggered backwards, winded.

'Crikey, Flora! Watch where you're going, can't you?' exclaimed Tan. 'I was running so fast I couldn't stop! What on earth are you doing here anyway? Your mum's going demented. She thinks you're late back from school!'

Flora hadn't time for explanations.

'Tan! Thank goodness! Look, go back to the house and get your dad. Joss' brother has got her and I don't know what he's going to do! I must get back to the canal!'

She turned to run but Tan caught her arm.

'Wait, Flora! What are you talking about? Slow down and tell me properly.'

Almost dancing up and down with agitation, Flora explained.

'I've got to go and see she's all right!' she finished, urgently. 'You just go and get David!'

'But what about... I mean, he might have to get the police. And he'll have to tell Libby. She's in the house. Flora, we've still got a day left to think of something!'

'Oh, shut up Tan!' snapped Flora. 'If I have to go to school, so what? That's better than leaving Joss to get beaten up!'

With that Flora was gone, pounding back to the towpath. She paused, her breath coming in noisy, give-away rasps, and peered anxiously along the canal, past the rhododendrons to where she expected Joss and Alex to be. But no one was there.

She screamed silently. Why couldn't Tan have been

quicker to understand? Well, they couldn't have gone far. But which way?

Flora calculated rapidly. What might have happened? Alex might have dragged Joss off somewhere. Or Joss might have got away from him. Either way, they wouldn't have gone towards the village or across the fields, for fear of being seen. Which left the tunnel.

20

Flora didn't hesitate. She had thought about herself enough. She dived into the tunnel.

A few metres of twilight and then inky darkness. It was an unusually long tunnel, considering it had a tow-path, and was far from welcoming. Flora could just see the little semi-circle of light in the distance but what would she find before she reached it? She groped her way along as quickly as she could but it was impossible to go very fast. Some ancient survival instinct kept her head bowed and her feet cautious, although she knew from exploring with a torch that the arch was high and the tow-path uncluttered. She strained her ears to hear Alex and Joss but the scuffling of her own feet and the steady drip-drip of water seeping through the roof echoed so loudly that it was hard to distinguish anything else.

She had to hurry. Already it felt as though she had been in the tunnel a very long time and the end seemed no nearer. She forced herself to speed up. Her mind held a terrifying picture of Alex dragging a struggling Joss away to his lair and however fiercely she told herself to be sensible, she was tormented by horrifying questions. Would he starve her until she did what he asked? Was he part of a desperate gang? Would he—awful thought—lose control and kill her? And what was she, Flora, doing, following him into this black trap? How would the others know which way she had gone? Alex could be waiting at the mouth of the tunnel even now, listening to her faltering footfalls, ready to pounce.

Flora stopped. She was being completely stupid. She should never have come in here on her own. Libby would go demented. For years she had been trying to protect Flora from mad axe men, and now here she was, following a complete stranger of her own accord. She should go back!

Flora screwed up her eyes, trying to work out how much further she had to go. Just as she did so, the semi-circle of light ahead seemed to shrink at one side—the tow-path side—and then, almost immediately, it resumed its former neat shape. Someone had just left the tunnel in a hurry—but who?

Her eyes now fixed rigidly ahead, Flora stumbled on. Who had it been? Was it Alex, making a quick get away, having dumped Joss' body in the canal? *Don't be stupid!* Flora told herself, fiercely. *It could just have been Joss running away.*

At that moment it happened again. A bigger bulge of blackness distorted the arch of light and, in her sudden stillness, Flora heard a man's voice in the distance.

'Joss! Joss! Stop!'

So Joss had got away! Flora broke into a jog, her head aching with its determination to stay bent.

Run! she urged Joss, mentally. *Run! We're coming to help you!*

At last Flora was standing, panting, in the mouth of the tunnel. But there was no time to catch her breath. The land dropped away dramatically here and hard on the tunnel entrance was the first of a short flight of locks. Flora ran to the top of the steps alongside it. Not very far away, just beyond the second lock, she could see Joss stumbling along, obviously at the end of her strength. Only metres behind her, almost at the lock-gate, was Alex. Away in the distance was a narrow boat, but Alex would have caught Joss long before that arrived.

Flora began to run. Perhaps she and Joss could fight off Alex together. At the very least she must keep them in sight! She just hoped help would arrive soon. How long was it since she had sent Tan running back to Buxton House?

Alex was at the top of the lock steps. Joss was flailing along the tow-path. She looked as if she had a bad stitch. Seconds now, and he would have her. Without thinking about it, Flora opened her mouth and yelled.

'Alex! STOP!'

Alex turned, startled. The steps were old, moss-covered and uneven and he lost his footing. For a split second Flora watched in amazement as Alex clawed at the air, and then he disappeared with a loud splash.

The next moment, Joss was hobbling back along the tow-path as if the hounds of hell were after her. Seeing Flora above her, frozen with horror, she screamed, 'Help me, for God's sake! He can't swim!'

Flora ran as she had never run before in her life. She knew only too well that the cut by the steps was far too deep for them to haul him out.

'O God! God!' she gasped. 'Help me! It'll be my fault if he drowns!'

Already Joss had stripped off most of her clothes and was lowering herself carefully into the canal, where the tow-path edge was close to the water level.

'Find a lifebelt!' she shouted.

'I'm not stupid!' snapped Flora, who knew perfectly well that swimming to help him before throwing a lifebelt would be a very bad idea. But how could she argue after what she had done? At least Joss had had the sense not to jump straight in.

It was only a matter of moments before Flora was lowering a lifebelt down the side of the steps. Joss was treading water and struggling to keep Alex up, whilst urging him to stay calm and keep his mouth shut.

When, after what seemed like forever, Alex's hands clasped the ring, Flora felt so faint with relief that the rope fell slack in her hands. She swayed slightly and would have fallen, but at that moment, strong hands steadied her and David said, 'It's all right, Flora. I've got the rope.'

She sat down with a bump and watched dazedly as Tan and David began to haul Alex along the deep cut to where they could help him out. In the distance she could hear a police siren. Exhausted, her head sank between her knees.

'Flora! Thank God you're all right!'

Flora struggled to look up. It felt as if a thousand ton weight was holding her head down, she was so tired.

'Mum,' she mumbled. 'Where… What…?'

'I came through the tunnel. We didn't wait for the police. We knew it'd take them a while to get here. Tan and David came straight across the fields. Thank goodness they did! Flora, I felt like strangling you when Tan got back to Buxton House! Don't you know how much you mean to me? Don't you realize I'd die if anything happened to you?'

'I'm sorry, Mum,' said Flora, and then Libby took her in her arms and they both cried together.

A short distance away, his head in his hands, sat Alex, his shoulders shaking violently. Tan wished he could find something warmer than his own sweatshirt and David's denim jacket to wrap round him—and he wished the ambulance which the police had sent for would hurry up and arrive. The sound of Alex alternately sobbing and retching was so unbearable that it physically hurt to listen. Close by, silent and white-faced, Joss was struggling into her clothes and David was deep in conversation with the two policemen who had arrived. Tan had never felt more awkward in his life. He was sure he ought to try to comfort Alex, or at least say *something* but the effort of speaking would have choked him.

With fumbling fingers, Joss tied her last lace. She straightened up and Tan watched as the terrible battle inside distorted her features. She walked slowly towards Alex, crouched down beside him and laid a hand on his shoulder.

'It's going to be all right, Alex,' she said. 'I still love you.'

With a terrible cry, Alex turned and clung to her, soaking her clothes and dwarfing her slender body.

Crikey! thought Tan, looking away. Alex, like his father Reuben, was a very big man. What he might have done if he had caught Joss in his anger didn't bear thinking about. The glimpse he had had of Joss' white face, tight against Alex's shoulder, told him that very much the same thought was passing through her mind. Tan felt sick.

'All right?' said David, putting an arm round Tan's shoulder.

Tan shook his head. 'Bit shaky,' he said. 'What's going to happen?'

'Not a lot,' said David. 'An ambulance is coming for Alex and Joss, but it's only a precaution. Alex might need his stomach pumped—depends how much canal water he drank. As far as the police are concerned, we're a bit of a waste of public money. I mean, what have we got to show them? A bloke and a kid who've been for a dip in the canal.'

'Yes, but they don't realize…'

'Perhaps it's best if they don't. How would Joss feel if Alex was dragged off by the police?'

'But he could have…'

'But he didn't. We don't know what would have happened. What we do know is that Alex needs help.'

'Yes,' said Tan, glancing over to where Alex was still huddled in Joss' arms. 'He certainly does.'

21

Stanley Hobbs did what he always did before he went home. He checked his diary for the next day. It was going to be busy. Hmm. Could he really fit in a visit to Flora Adams' mother? Yes, he could. After all it was probably only going to be a quick check. The letter he had received looked genuine enough.

Dear Mr Hobbs, it had said.

Thank you for your concern about Flora. For the time being, she is continuing her education at home as I still have not found a school which I feel is suitable. I very much hope that the situation will be sorted out before long. Thank you.

Yours sincerely,

Elizabeth Adams (Ms)

But he ought to check, just to be on the safe side. And it ought to be pointed out to Ms Adams that the longer she left it before choosing a new school, the more difficult it would be for Flora to settle in. Yes. He would squeeze in a visit tomorrow morning. It wouldn't take long.

The ambulance had gone. The police had gone. David had gone to tell Zilla and give her a lift to the hospital. Libby hurried Tan and Flora back to Buxton House, where she made them drink mugs of sweet tea

141

and fed them digestive biscuits before sending Flora off to relax in the bath whilst she phoned for a pizza.

Then she turned to Tan.

'I never did find out why Flora was so late back from school,' she said. 'Do you have any idea, Tan?'

Tan fidgeted uncomfortably and then made up his mind. 'I do,' he said, meeting her eyes bravely. 'But I'm not going to tell you. It's up to Flora.'

'Oh, come on, Tan!' Libby sounded impatient.

'No,' said Tan.

And Libby knew that he wasn't going to budge.

'OK then,' she said. 'I'll ask Flora.'

But at that moment, David got back from the hospital and, in the flurry of questioning about Joss and Alex, Flora was forgotten. It wasn't until David was driving them back home, much later, that Libby remembered again.

'David, I never did find out what happened to Flora,' she said.

There was a sharp little gasp from the back seat.

'Oh, leave it till tomorrow, love,' David said, easily. 'I'm sure it wasn't anything too awful.'

Libby pulled a face. 'Something tells me you all know something I don't,' she said, 'but I'm too exhausted to worry about it.'

So was Flora, but that didn't stop her. She had lain in the bath and worried about it; she had barely touched her pizza for worrying about it. She knew that if she didn't say something soon, she wouldn't be able to sleep for worrying about it. It seemed quite incredible that, after all that had happened, Libby still didn't know that Flora hadn't come home from school that afternoon because she had never gone.

Fear had stopped her mouth all evening. Fear of Libby's anger, fear that the very next day she might be back on the school bus, surrounded by mocking children, fear that her life would return to an endless round of misery, migraine and eczema.

Without realizing it, she began to scratch.

'Flora!' hissed Tan from the other end of the back seat. 'Stop it!'

Flora stopped immediately, horrified. No! She would not scratch herself raw over this. That was precisely what she wanted to escape from. OK, so she was frightened. Scared stiff, in fact. So? She had been frightened before and survived. What about the morning she had crouched breathless in the undergrowth, terrified that a little dog was about to give her away? What about the time when she had thought David was about to march her home from the den and tell Libby everything? What about today, when she had followed Joss and Alex into the tunnel? Was she still just a scabby little drip? *Do whatever you think is best.* David's words had haunted her long enough. As soon as she was alone with Libby, she would confess everything. Perhaps, once again, she could try asking God for help—this God who David claimed was on the side of truth.

'Mum,' she said, when they were back on the *Thorpe Cloud* and David and Tan had gone. 'About this afternoon…'

'Oh, Flora, let's leave that till tomorrow morning, shall we?' yawned Libby. 'I'm absolutely exhausted and I'm sure you must be too—and no harm's done after all. It's just as well you were there, as it turns out.'

'But Mum…'

'No, Flora, I insist. We'll talk about it in the morning.

'What we both need right now is a good night's sleep.'

Flora lay in her bunk, staring at the ceiling which was so low she could have reached out and touched it. A good night's sleep, huh? Every time she closed her eyes, she seemed to be back in the tunnel, anxiously groping her way through. And she was worried about Joss and Alex. What was going to happen? Joss had been sent home from hospital that evening but Alex had been kept in overnight. He was expected home in the morning. What would Zilla and Reuben do with him? Was he safe?

But more than anything else, of course, she was awake because she had to talk to Libby. Having made up her mind to do it, it was agony to put it off till the morning. More than once she thought of padding through and waking her mum but the thought of telling a tired, grumpy, half-asleep Libby was even more awful than lying awake all night. It was getting towards dawn before she finally fell into an uneasy slumber, in which she dreamed endlessly of searching for lifebelts, all of which turned into giant pizzas as soon as she picked them up.

Stanley Hobbs studied his road map. He had a few spot checks to do that morning and his time was precious. He needed to plan a sensible route. He would visit Flora Adams first. He just hoped the *Thorpe Cloud* wasn't too far along the tow-path. He'd once made a visit to a narrow boat which was moored half a mile from the nearest road. Oh well. It was a pleasant morning for a walk.

'Come on, Flora, wake up!' Libby was shaking her

gently. 'It's late and you ought to have something to eat.'

Flora groaned and opened an eye. Why did she feel so rough? Her eyes hurt and her tongue tasted rancid. Then she remembered.

'Mum,' she said, blearily. 'Mum, I've got to talk to you.'

'Plenty of time for that, Flora. I'm keeping you at home today. Get dressed and have some breakfast first. I'm just popping out to see Zilla.'

Flora pulled on some jeans and a sweatshirt, screwed up with frustration that, now that she had plucked up the courage to tell Libby the truth, she kept finding excuses not to be told.

It was a good half-hour before Libby was back from the *Argo*.

'Well,' she said, as soon as she was down the steps. 'Alex is much better this morning and...'

'Mum,' Flora interrupted in an imploring voice. 'Please. I've got something I simply have to tell you...'

Fifteen minutes later, Flora sat with her head in her hands whilst Libby filled the *Thorpe Cloud* with her rage. It was at least as bad as Flora had expected. Furious words zinged about her like firecrackers.

'How dare you, my only child, deceive me so flagrantly—and for so long? And Tan! What was he *thinking* of to help you to do it? Lying to your school like that! And to send letters! To actually write letters, full of your lies! How *could* you? I shall speak to David. I shall speak to him in the strongest possible way. I shall tell him where educating his son at home has got him. I shall...'

145

'But Mum,' wailed Flora. 'It wasn't Tan's fault. He was only trying to help!'

'To help? A child already falling behind at school taking several weeks off to skulk around in his den? Is that going to help? I don't think so!'

'But, Mum, it has, honestly it has. I can read now, I can write—it's made such a difference. Please believe me.'

But Libby wasn't listening.

'What on earth am I going to say to the school when I take you back? Because, make no mistake, it's back to school you go, young lady. What sort of mother will they think I am? I'll probably have social workers and educational welfare officers and goodness knows who else prying into our concerns! What a mess you have got us into, you and Tan together!'

At that moment there was a knock on the cabin door. Libby didn't hear it, she was so distracted. It came again.

Flora got up. 'There's someone at the door, Mum,' she said quietly.

'What?' said Libby, looking quite wild about the eyes. 'Well, they can go away and come back later, can't they?'

But the door was not locked and had been pushed open slightly.

'I am sorry to disturb you,' said a polite but firm voice, 'but I wonder if you could spare me a few minutes of your time? I'm Stanley Hobbs, the Educational Welfare Officer.'

I don't believe it, thought Flora, faintly.

'You see!' Libby almost spat and flopped down in a chair with a groan.

Oh God! thought Flora. *Why didn't I tell her last week?*

Flora led the way along the tow-path. She couldn't quite believe what was happening. From behind she could still hear little bursts of indignant speech as Libby thought of more and more things to be furious about.

'Yes, I do see,' said Stanley Hobbs, patiently. 'Yes, I take your point.'

Flora thought he must be very used to coping with ranting mums and dads. Libby alternately raged and apologized, but he behaved as if discovering children choosing to home-educate themselves was an everyday event—a little blip which could easily be dealt with. His polite matter-of-factness did a lot to calm Libby down. When she had finally run out of steam, he said, 'I wonder, if it's not putting you to too much trouble, if I could have a cup of tea? And then perhaps Flora could show us some of the work she's been doing all this time with Tan. Was that his name?'

Flora nodded. 'It's a nick-name for Nathaniel,' she explained. 'All my work is in his den. But I can show you how well I can read now.'

Libby snorted.

'Please, Ms Adams,' said Stanley Hobbs, for the first time sounding slightly annoyed. 'I would love to hear you read, Flora.'

Flora hurried to fetch *A Little Princess* whilst Libby made some tea. Surely her mum would be impressed to hear her read from that?

Only the gentle lapping of the water against the boat broke the silence as she read. Hearing her own voice filling the whole cabin was so scary that Flora almost stopped. But she didn't. As she read on her heart began to lift until by the end of the chapter she could have sung the words, she was so elated. Libby must believe in her now!

There was a little silence when she finished.

'Thank you, Flora,' said Stanley Hobbs. 'That was beautifully read.'

Flora looked at her mother who had a look of dazed wonder on her face. Her mug of tea was untouched. 'I have read it to her several times, Mr Hobbs,' she said, hesitantly, 'but…'

'Surely you're not suggesting Flora could have remembered it all?' he interrupted.

'No… no,' said Libby, obviously completely baffled. 'I just…'

'Well, Ms Adams, may I be so bold as to suggest that as soon as you've finished your tea, we go along to Flora's den and see what else she's been up to?'

'Yes,' said Libby in a blank voice. 'Yes. I think perhaps we'd better.'

Tan was footling about in David's studio, unable to settle to anything. He longed to go down to the *Thorpe Cloud* to see Flora and to find out what had happened to Joss and Alex, but David wouldn't let him.

'Go a bit later,' he said. 'Give them a chance to catch their breath. Both Flora and Libby were absolutely shattered last night. If they feel anything like I do this morning, they won't want you blundering in.'

He was just wondering whether he had waited long enough and David would let him go, when a movement outside caught his eye. Tan walked to the big windows and looked out.

It was Flora leading the way to the den. Behind her were Libby and a man he didn't recognize. But he knew at once who it must be.

'Dad!' he shouted, as he rushed out of the room and ran down the stairs. 'Dad! Come quickly! Flora needs us!'

'It's the Educational Welfare Officer, I'm sure it is,' gasped Tan, hopping up and down in the doorway of the kitchen. 'Oh, come on, Dad. You've got to come and tell him how well she's been doing. He's never going to believe me!'

'I'm sure he can see for himself, Tan,' said David, calmly. 'He's hardly likely to be an ogre. Three minutes and the flapjack will be out of the oven. I'll come then, OK? Go yourself if you think he's going to eat her.'

Tan thought about the letters he had helped Flora to write, especially the last one which she didn't even know about.

'I think I'll wait for you,' he said.

Tan thought he would burst with impatience as David carefully marked out the flapjack into squares and set it to cool, but at last he was ready.

At the door of the den, Tan stopped.

'Well?' said David. 'It's your den.'

With a hand clammy with nerves, Tan turned the handle and opened the door.

'Ah, hello,' said a friendly-looking man with one of Flora's books in his hand. 'You, I take it, must be Tan.'

22

Twenty minutes later everyone was sitting round the huge kitchen table in Buxton House, munching warm, sticky chunks of flapjack.

'Well,' said Stanley Hobbs, cheerfully, who had long ago given up all thought of making any more visits that morning. 'This is a nice bonus.'

'We thought you would be horrid,' said Flora, unguardedly.

'I can be,' he admitted, 'but who could be horrid eating such delicious flapjack?'

'We told a lot of lies,' said Tan, blushing.

'Ah,' said Stanley Hobbs, looking at him in a very piercing way. 'Fortunately it isn't my job to deal with that. I'm just here to sort out Flora's academic education.'

'Which you haven't done yet,' said Libby.

'Correction,' replied the officer, licking his fingers. 'Which *you* haven't done yet.'

'But I don't *know* what to do!' wailed Libby. 'Of course I can see how well she's been getting on in the den—in fact, apart from all the lying, I've never been so proud of her in my life—I never realized she had such guts. But she can't carry on like that! She ought to be with other kids—and going on outings—oh, there's all sorts of stuff she'd miss out on just holed up in that shed! And I certainly can't educate her myself. I have to earn a living.'

David cleared his throat. 'I think you're missing the obvious, Libby,' he said.

'Oh no you don't,' said Libby. 'I know what you're going to say and there's no way I can say yes. It would be too much to ask. You couldn't possibly.'

'But why not, Libby? She's managed perfectly well on her own with absolutely no input from me. It's hardly going to be a huge burden.'

'But what about when she's older? What about GCSEs and all that?'

David shrugged. 'We could cross that bridge when we come to it. Who knows? She might want to try school by then.'

Flora was nearly jumping up and down with frustration. 'What are you *talking* about? You're talking about me as if I'm not here—but I am and I want to know what you mean!'

Tan laughed. 'Oh, Flora. Isn't it obvious? Dad's offering to educate you himself!'

'Oo-oh!' said Flora. She met David's eyes and then looked away quickly. Her cheeks flamed hot and uncomfortable. Of course, she had thought about it— dreamed about it even, in those first days in the den. But now? After all that had passed between them?

David stood up. 'Excuse us,' he said. 'I think Flora and I need a quick chat. We won't be long, I promise. OK, Flora?'

Unwillingly Flora got up and followed him out of the room. Now wasn't the time to argue.

David led the way out onto the tow-path and sat down on the grass by the tunnel. Awkwardly, leaving a large gap between them, Flora did the same.

'How about it then, Flora?' said David, looking sideways at her. 'Have you forgiven me yet?'

Flora kicked at a stray piece of gravel. 'There's nothing to forgive,' she said, grumpily.

David said nothing.

'None of it's your fault,' Flora continued in a hard little voice. 'You didn't find out about me deliberately. And you didn't have a chance to split on us.'

'But I did fall in love with Libby. I do want to marry her.'

'You're crazy,' said Flora, angrily. 'You should see her when she gets mad! And she's terribly impatient—and dreadfully untidy.'

'But *you* love her.'

'I *have* to. She's all I've got.'

Flora's words hung accusingly in the silence and she stared stonily at the floor.

David stood up and put his hands in his pockets. 'Oh well,' he said. 'That's that, then. If that's the way you feel. The offer's still open though. Sorry it's not a great choice—school or me—but I can't think of anything else right now.'

He turned and began to go back to the house.

Flora fought the hardest battle of her life. 'Dear God,' she whimpered, 'I want to do the right thing!'

David was opening the door of the kitchen by the time Flora, panting, had caught up with him.

'Stop!' she yelled. 'Wait a minute!'

David turned and was almost flattened as Flora threw herself across the hall and into his arms.

'I'm sorry,' she sobbed into his jumper. 'I couldn't

help it. I've been so jealous and mean and selfish. But it's all right now—really it is.'

David crouched down and held Flora against him.

'It isn't really fair though, is it?' he said, gently. 'Me and everything that goes with me or school? It's not a real choice. D'you want to think about it some more?'

Flora looked into his face. 'I've thought about it,' she said, managing a smile through her tears. 'I've been thinking about it for weeks. You and Libby, I mean. It isn't fair to be so jealous. And anyway, you've got to be better than school.'

'Thanks,' said David. 'Damned with faint praise.'

'What's that mean?' sniffed Flora.

'It means I'd never have recovered from the insult if you'd chosen school.'

There was a pause.

'Libby can love both of us, you know,' said David, quietly.

'I know that really,' said Flora.

'So shall I ask her to marry me?'

Flora's wet face broke into a mischievous grin and she hugged David hard.

'Do whatever you think is best,' she said.

Later that afternoon, Flora stood on the tow-path outside the *Argo*.

'Go on,' said Tan. 'I'll wait here.'

'I might be ages,' said Flora, dubiously.

'So what? I've got a book to read. If I get really fed up, I can always go and irritate your mum and my dad. They're so lovey-dovey I want to throw up.'

Flora laughed and then strode up the *Argo*'s gangplank.

Joss was lying on the bunk in her room. She sat up when Flora came in.

'Hello,' she said, bleakly.

Flora took a deep breath. She knew what she had to do.

'I've come to say I'm sorry,' she said.

'What for?'

Joss' voice wasn't exactly encouraging but Flora carried on, doggedly.

'Everything,' she said, firmly. 'For saying those stupid things when you told me about the boat yard, for going off with Tan and forgetting you, for ignoring you for weeks when I knew something was wrong, for slapping you, for making you write all those notes when I skived off school…'

'I didn't have to write them…' said Joss, irritably biting her fingernails.

Flora thought about it. She thought about the way she had whined and wheedled and even cried. Anyone with a heart would have given in. When she looked back she realized she had been abusing Joss' friendship for ages.

She shook her head. 'You did,' she said. 'And it was my fault. I'm sorry.'

Joss continued gnawing her fingernails. Flora could see her face working as she struggled to find something to say.

'It's no good!' she suddenly burst out. 'I can't say it's all right! I know the boat yard's going to be saved and Alex is getting sorted out and you did the right thing when you went to get help. But you made me so jealous, the way you suddenly took up with Tan and then you just kept on ignoring me—I never thought you meant it when you said you'd never speak to me again!'

'But...' Flora thought of all the things Joss had said. They were still written sky-high in her memory. *Smarty-pants*. *Wimp*. *A scabby little drip*. She had to clench her fists tightly and take a very firm grip of herself. No! There was no point in going over all that. She wasn't there to start another row.

'I was angry too,' she said, honestly. 'I said some terrible things. I'm sorry.'

'OK,' said Joss, stiffly. 'I accept your apology.'

Flora felt winded. Was that it? Was that all she was going to say? Wasn't she going to say sorry for any of the things *she* had said? Was she going to allow Flora to take all the blame? She waited but Joss only chewed her nails down even further.

Well, Flora could storm out now. That's what she felt like doing. But what good would that do? They'd be back to square one, their friendship in tatters. It dawned on Flora that it was entirely up to her. Joss wasn't ready to say sorry; she wasn't even really ready to forgive. If Flora wanted to rebuild their friendship, she was going to have to work very hard. It would be a long, long time before they were as close as they had been—if ever. Unless Joss met her half-way.

Flora sighed heavily. All the hope and determination she had felt as she strode onto the *Argo* seemed to have melted away. Was it worth it?

'Well?' said Joss, suddenly breaking the silence. 'Don't you want to hear about Alex?'

Flora shook herself. 'Of course,' she said, rather too brightly. 'Sorry. I was miles away. Is he all right? I can't wait to hear the whole story.'

'There's not much to tell,' said Joss, with a sigh. 'You know he got put away for joyriding?'

'Well, I knew he'd gone to prison.'

'Not prison, silly. He was too young. One of those young offenders' places—that's where he went.'

'Oh,' said Flora. She hadn't realized there was a difference.

'Well, he hated it. It was totally overcrowded and he was banged up with all these awful people—real criminals, even if they were only young.'

'But…' Flora had been going to say something about Alex being a real criminal too but hastily changed her mind.

'Anyway,' continued Joss, 'once he'd been sentenced, he decided he was never going to let himself get stuck in there again—so he got himself on this course to train to be a car mechanic.'

'What? Whilst he was in prison?'

'Oh, yeah,' said Joss, casually. 'There's all sorts of stuff you can do. They want people to come out straight, don't they?'

'Oh,' said Flora. She really had no idea. 'So what happened then?'

'Well, he was OK for a bit,' said Joss. 'But it's all gone wrong again.'

'Why?'

'Well, he got a job at a small garage and learned absolutely masses about mending cars—but in the end, he got fed up. He wanted his own business—to be his own boss.'

'But wouldn't he need a lot of money for that?'

'He didn't think so—not if he started small. He reckoned he could rent a little workshop—he'd been saving like mad—and he knew enough people in the trade to get going. He didn't expect to make a fortune—just enough to live off.'

'But it didn't work?'

'No—he's been falling behind with the rent on the workshop—but he was desperate to keep going. That's why he came to find me. He hasn't spoken to Mum and Dad for years. Not since the last time he got caught joyriding. And anyway he'd heard about the boat yard—he knew it wasn't a good time to come asking for money.'

'So you started taking all that stuff—and he sold it?'

Joss nodded fiercely. 'It wasn't really stealing because it all belonged to us anyway. Wouldn't you have done the same? For your brother?'

'I haven't got a brother,' said Flora, simply.

They looked at each other in silence.

'You even sold your flute,' said Flora, quietly. She still couldn't quite believe it.

Joss nodded and looked away. Flora knew she was struggling not to cry.

'You must love him an awful lot,' Flora said. She considered her own jealous love for Libby and thought she understood.

'So what's going to happen now?' she asked.

Joss blew her nose. 'He's agreed to see a doctor because he's so depressed. And a debt counsellor to help him sort out his money problems. And Mum and Dad think they might be able to help him a bit with the rent. The boat yard plans are going ahead, so it should be OK. They still can't do much—but maybe just enough to keep him on his feet for a while. It's about time they did something for him—they never understood him when he was a kid.'

'It wasn't their fault,' said Flora, defensively, thinking of kindly Zilla and Reuben.

'Then whose fault was it?' demanded Joss, in a hard, churlish voice.

'I don't know,' said Flora, 'but I don't think it's fair to blame them.'

Flora wanted to go home. It was too depressing. She had wanted to say sorry to Joss and for it all to be better. But it wasn't as simple as that. There were too many other things to sort out. Suddenly Joss' life, which she had always envied, was awful—and her own seemed to have taken a joyous turn for the better. Why? Why? Why? Why had everything changed?

Her eczema was much better. She was learning how to deal with her migraines. She knew that Libby loved her as well as David. She wasn't going to go back to school. And Tan, who would still be sitting waiting for her, had become as good a friend as Joss had ever been. It was enough to make her giddy with joy.

But she still loved Joss.

Flora looked at her, sitting glumly on the bed, and cleared her throat.

'Can't we still be friends, Joss?' she said, bravely. 'I really am sorry about everything that's happened.'

'I *said* it was OK,' said Joss, irritably. Then, just as Flora was feeling it was completely hopeless, Joss tossed her hair aside and looked at her properly for the first time since she had come in. She half-smiled. 'Of course we're still friends,' she said.

'Well?' said Tan, looking up from the book he was reading as he squatted on the grassy bank. 'How did it go? Are you friends again?'

Flora shook her head. 'Not like before,' she said, sadly. 'I said I was sorry and she said it was OK but she didn't mean it. She's still mad with me. And she wouldn't say sorry to me for anything.'

'Oh well,' said Tan, dusting the grass from his jeans. 'You've done your bit.'

'Yes, but it isn't enough,' said Flora, crossly.

'Well, what else can you do? Except wait and see.'

'I suppose so. She said we were still friends.'

'Well then...'

'I know, I know—but it isn't the same...'

They dawdled on up the tow-path in silence.

'I suppose I could try praying,' said Flora, at last.

Tan laughed. 'Oh yeah? You're getting very holy.'

Flora gave him a half-hearted push. 'Shut up, you idiot. You said there was no harm in trying. So I am. What's wrong with that?'

'Nothing,' said Tan. 'It's fine by me. I just hope you know what you're doing. I don't want God sending any thunderbolts.'

Flora glowered at him. 'I'll order one specially,' she said. 'All my other prayers have worked.'

'Really? So how come my dad's marrying your mum? I always thought you couldn't bear the idea.'

'I never prayed that they wouldn't! And how do you know how I felt, anyway? I never said anything.'

'Just guessed you felt the same way as me,' said Tan, casually. He wasn't looking at her and for a moment Flora didn't quite take in what he'd said. She had to re-play it a couple of times.

'Oh,' she said suddenly and stood stock-still. Never, until that moment, had she thought about how Tan might feel, so lost had she been in her own troubles.

Now it was blindingly obvious. Why should Tan feel any different? Why should he want to share David? Or have Libby for a mum?

Tan was several strides ahead of her. 'Tan,' Flora called. 'Tan, wait! I'm sorry. I never thought...'

He stopped and smiled back at her. 'It's all right now, you know,' he said. 'I've got used to the idea.'

'Really? You're not just saying that?'

''Course not. Anyway, I've always wanted a little sister.'

He waited, grinning, whilst her mouth dropped open. Then, before she had a chance to catch him and push him in the canal, he turned and hared off towards Buxton House.